SACRIFICIAL GROUNDS

The Bell Witch Series Book 2

Written by Sara Clancy
Edited by Kathryn St. John-Shin

ISBN: 9781086344073
Copyright © 2019 by ScareStreet.com

THANK YOU AND BONUS NOVEL!

I'd like to take a moment to thank you for your ongoing support. You make this all possible! To really show you my appreciation for purchasing this book, **I'd love to send you a full-length horror novel in 3 formats (MOBI, EPUB and PDF) absolutely free!**

Download your full-length horror novel, get free short stories, and receive future discounts by visiting www.ScareStreet.com/SaraClancy

See you in the shadows,
Sara Clancy

CHAPTER 1

Campfire smoke and forest pine lingered in the warm Spring breeze. Only a few months ago, Mina would have found it a pleasant smell. Now, each breath threatened to summon a flood of memories she would sooner forget.

Tales of the Bell Witch had filled her childhood. She had never believed them. Even now, she was sure that superstition and fear had mutated individual 'facts' beyond recognition. But she could no longer doubt there was far more truth to it than she had ever suspected. She had lived through the Harvest; those last days of October when the Bell Witch selected a person from each of the four families she had damned, and lured them back to where it had all started. The backwoods of Black River, Tennessee. The Witch Woods.

A screaming child sprinted across her field of vision. Mina jerked, her shoulder slamming against the side of Basheba's car as the child cut across the campsite. Basheba glared at the kid until it jumped into the nearby lake and disappeared within the turquoise water.

"I hate Spring Break," Basheba muttered as she returned to prodding the campfire to make the flames grow.

They were the first words Basheba had spoken in the last twenty minutes and Mina was eager to extend it into a full conversation.

"Because of all the kids?"

Basheba arched an eyebrow but went back to tending her fire without a word. Under five feet tall, blonde, and with skin like strawberries and cream, Basheba Bell looked like a porcelain doll, not a woman in her twenties with a violent fear of children. Even the leather patch covering her left eye couldn't change that.

"How's your eye?" Mina asked, studying the eyepatch with a mix of awe and guilt.

The Bell Witch hadn't been the only one to underestimate Basheba and the lengths to which she was willing to go. Mina had thought herself as good as dead when the Witch had manifested the key behind Basheba's eye. Everyone else had already locked their demon boxes, and the two girls had clashed from the beginning. But Basheba hadn't hesitated. There, laying in the snow and muck, covered in blood and without anesthetic, she had ordered Cadwyn to cut out her eye.

Over the months, Mina had thought of that moment so often she could recall every second in detail. Cadwyn Winthrop was a career psych nurse in a maximum-security prison. It was kind of a waste. He had the hands of a surgeon. With only a basic medical pack, he had skillfully removed Basheba's eye, retrieved the key, and returned the orb to its socket without causing any lasting damage. His expertise didn't end there. Somehow, he had managed to keep infection at bay for the entire two-day hike back to town. If Mina hadn't been afraid of Basheba before, the fact that she walked the whole way without a word of complaint would have done it.

"Had a check-up this morning," Basheba answered at last. "I've got to wear the patch for a few more weeks. After that, I'll just have to do the odd exercise to keep the muscle strong."

"Any visual damage?"

"None." A small smile curled the edges of her lips. "I knew Cadwyn could do it. I'm not going to lie; I really want to rub it in Katrina's smug face."

Mina flinched. When people spoke of the Witch, it was always by her title and with a certain degree of reverent fear, like she was some malicious god. For Basheba, however, the Witch was nothing more than a pathetic hag with delusions of grandeur. She called her by name. Either spitting it out with undiluted contempt or lingering on it with mockery. Mina couldn't decide if she found it unnerving or comforting. *Maybe it's different for the Bells*, Mina thought. *They've lived with her the longest.*

Katrina's obsession with the Bells had been her destruction. It had exposed her as a witch and brought about her execution. But even death hadn't been enough to stop her. She hated them with a rage so potent it had bled out to consume four bloodlines for two hundred years. She was The *Bell* Witch.

"My first year of college has been fun," Mina blurted out. Basheba might be immune to awkward silences, but she wasn't. "Busy, but fun."

"Criminal Justice, right?" Basheba asked absently.

"Yeah. It's a huge workload, but I was prepared for that. It's the extracurriculars. Between moot court, volunteering at the hospital, and the soup kitchen, I barely have time to think."

Basheba paused and turned to her.

Mina shrugged. "I need a free ride to Harvard Med. The competition is intense. You need to stand out."

Basheba's brow furrowed but she quickly hid her reaction. "You have a free ride now, right?"

"Full scholarship," Mina beamed, puffing up a little with pride.

Mina had written down her life plan when she was in kindergarten. From there, no matter how hard she worked, it felt like she was just waiting for her life to begin. Now she was on track. Her Criminal Justice degree was in sight. She'd use it to secure her medical degree. Then it would be straight to the Federal Bureau of Investigation.

"And that covers dorm room?"

Mina deflated somewhat. "It did, but I'm staying with my cousin."

"Why?"

"My parents offered to pay for my living expenses if I did. I don't have time for a part-time job. It only makes sense."

Basheba opened her mouth as if to speak, but then seemed to decide in the last moment to keep it to herself and went back to tending her fire, waiting for her kettle to boil. Buck, Basheba's colossal Rottweiler, grumbled as he shuffled closer to Mina's knees. His slick tongue flopped out to lap at his jaws. There was something in the motion that Mina took as a threat. Buck adored Basheba and rarely ventured more than a few feet from her side. This unwavering attention felt like he was obeying a command. In the woods, she'd seen just how savage he could be for his mistress.

The Witch had preyed on Basheba's odd fear of children, conjuring demons that looked just like them. Buck hadn't hesitated to rip through them in a storm of fangs and blood. Even if she had been spared the sight of the horrific aftermath, the sheer size of the Rottweiler was enough to leave people on edge. Mina watched families come and go, pulling up into the camping spaces next to Basheba's, only to move again after catching sight of the monstrous hound.

Barbeques were lit while Basheba worked on her tea, adding the scents of sizzling sausages to the lingering aroma. People played in the lake, splashing and squealing, while others wandered about, taking photographs of the surrounding mountains.

"This is a gorgeous spot," Mina said, hoping to reignite the conversation. "Have you been here before?"

"I don't go to the same place twice," Basheba dismissed, poking at the charred wood. It split with a pop, spewing embers up around the kettle.

"Nowhere?" Mina asked.

A few distant shrill screams of delight and the crackle of the fire was the only response Mina received. *My back is starting to hurt from carrying this conversation*, Mina thought with a small measure of bitterness. She had come here with a purpose, and couldn't broach the subject until she got Basheba into a good mood. *Maybe I should have started with Cadwyn.*

She frowned as she studied Basheba's car. A dented, old copper-colored Chevrolet hatchback that should have gone to the scrap heap after the Witch had totaled it. Apparently, Basheba had put a lot of the money Ozzie Sewall had given her into restoring it.

Davis, Mina corrected herself. Up until a few months ago, the poor guy hadn't even known he was biologically a Sewall, or of the curse he had inherited. His whole life, he had thought that Percival Sewall was his godfather and that he had been born a Davis. It was a lot to deal with, but the fifteen-year-old had held it together in the woods.

"Have you heard from Ozzie lately?" Mina asked.

It might help somewhat. Basheba had warmed up to him a bit.

"Yeah. His arm's fine."

"I thought he gave you money for a new car."

"My car works just fine. I used that for travel, instead," Basheba shrugged. "I don't think he'll mind."

"As the heir to *two* of the wealthiest families in the world, nah, I don't think he will," Mina giggled.

Basheba's brow furrowed slightly.

"They both made it onto the Forbes Top 100 list last year."

"Really?"

"I know, it's so weird, isn't it? I always thought people that rich were obligated to be jerks."

"No, I mean, you read Forbes Magazine?" Basheba shook her head in bafflement. "Weird."

Mina pressed her lips into a tight smile to keep from sighing. *This isn't going well.* She had memorized a few topics of conversation before approaching Basheba. It hadn't been an easy task. Four days in the woods alone and she still didn't know that much about the shorter girl. It was easy enough to tell what she hated. She never hid her rage. Against the families, the Witch, her uncle. Her disgust was bearded for all to see. But Mina wanted to put her in a good mood. That was harder. Beyond travel, the only things that brought a smile to her face were Buck, Cadwyn, and fire. *She brought up travel. Follow up on it.*

"Where did you go? With the extra cash?"

"Florida. I wanted to see the Everglades and go to Disney World." At last, the blonde smiled with real warmth. Not at Mina, but at Buck.

"Disney World?" Mina pressed, trying to regain the girl's attention.

Basheba hummed. "I prefer Dollywood."

"They let you on the rides with your eye in that condition?"

"No."

"Why didn't you wait? I mean, if you never go back to a place, it seems a bit of a waste."

Basheba stared at her like she was slow. "If I waited, my eye wouldn't have looked so gross."

"Yes, that's right," Mina said, still confused.

Basheba sighed heavily and pinched the bridge of her nose. "Well, they wouldn't let me bring in my service animal if I looked okay, right?"

Mina stammered as the kettle whistled. She studied Basheba carefully as the blonde poured out two cups of tea and came to sit beside her.

"You managed to convince them Buck was a service dog?"

It was a level of bravado Mina hadn't thought anyone was capable of reaching. The trunk of the hatchback car had been converted into a bed and, once she was seated upon the mattress, Basheba's legs were too short to reach the ground. She swung them absentmindedly as she handed Mina a mug.

"We've got under seven months until the next Harvest, and I wasn't about to go out without getting a pic of Buck and me with Cinderella."

Blindsided by another unexpected statement, Mina numbly took the mug. "Cinderella?"

"She's my favorite."

"*You* have a favorite princess?"

"Yeah."

"And it's *Cinderella*?"

"The girl was willing to walk on broken glass just to give the middle finger to her lifelong emotional abusers," Basheba sighed wistfully. "If only I could be that badass."

The memory of Basheba using a lighter and a can of antiseptic spray as a makeshift flamethrower flashed across Mina's mind.

"Personally, I find you terrifying." Mina hadn't meant for the words to slip out but was glad to see Basheba's growing smile.

"Aw, that's sweet. Drink your tea."

Warmth beamed from her smile even while her eyes remained as cold as a grave. It made Mina's skin crawl. *She's up to something.* Forcing a matching smile, Mina cupped the hot mug with both hands and nodded her thanks.

"Blow on it first. Don't want to burn yourself," Basheba chirped.

Mina took a tentative sip. It took a moment for the heat to fade and leave a sweet, lingering taste.

"This is nice," Mina said.

"Oh, good. I was worried I wouldn't brew it right," Basheba said. "I had to do your favorite blend justice, right?"

"Favorite blend?" Mina raised her mug to sniff at the steam. *Sweet berries.* But she couldn't place which kind.

"I just assumed it was," Basheba continued pleasantly, adding when Mina took another exploratory sip. "Why else would you bring the leaves into the woods with you?"

Mina lurched forward, spraying the contents out over her hand and lap. *Belladonna. I just drank Belladonna.*

"Too hot?" Basheba asked.

She glanced up at the blonde, absently wiping at her mouth. Basheba smiled.

"Drink your tea, Willimina."

"Basheba, that was Belladonna."

"I know."

"Deadly Nightshade," Mina pressed. "It's toxic. Have you been drinking this?"

"Of course not," Basheba chuckled. The sound came and went in a second, replaced by an icy glare. "Drink your tea."

What? "It's poison."

"Well, yeah. I'm murdering you. Honestly, how is it taking you this long to catch on? You're supposed to be smart."

For a long moment, Mina could only stare at her, brow furrowed and jaw hanging open. A thousand thoughts raced through her head, but she could only manage to stammer.

7

"You can't do that."

"Who's going to stop me?" Basheba said with clear amusement.

"I won't drink it."

"That's your choice," Basheba shrugged. "It's what I would do. But then, I always take the hard way."

"What?"

She got her answer when she stretched out her arm, ready to tip the contents on the grass. Buck's lips curled back as he released a low, rumbling growl. Long, pristine fangs glistened in the noonday light. Mina froze. She didn't expect the sharp lurch he took toward her. Forgetting about the cup, she threw herself back to escape his snapping jaws, making the steaming liquid slosh over her hand.

"Hey, don't wet my bed," Basheba protested.

Gathering her wits, Mina chuckled nervously. "You almost had me there. I honestly thought you were going to kill me."

"I am," Basheba replied. "Well, me or Buck. But there's no 'I' in team. A kill for one of us is a kill for both."

"You can't do this!"

"You keep saying that," Basheba dismissed.

Mina grappled for understanding, her heart racing and Bucks growling ringing in her ears.

"We're in public."

"So?"

"Dog attacks draw attention. People are concerned by that sort of thing."

"Yeah. And when people are concerned, they make sure their loved ones are safe first. Keys are in the ignition. It won't take long for him to rip out your throat. I think we can get away while they're trying to help you."

"You'll have to leave everything behind," Mina blurted.

"They're just things. All replaceable."

"We're not in Black River. Crimes have consequences here. You'll go to prison, and Buck will be put down."

Basheba tilted her head, seeming to consider that. At last, she shrugged. "We're five minutes from the state border. You'd be surprised what you can get away with just by crossing jurisdiction lines. Drink. Or stand. Your call."

The reality struck Mina like a wall of ice. Basheba Bell was completely willing to kill her. Here and now. After they had been chatting idly for at least twenty minutes. *Think,* she commanded herself as sweat beaded along her hairline. *Stay calm and think.*

"I never used it," Mina said, trying to buy some time for her mind to work.

"You didn't have time to," Basheba countered. "That doesn't count. You brought it along. One leaf for me. One for Cadwyn. One for Ozzie. None for you. The intention's pretty clear."

Cadwyn. A small idea blossomed on the edges of Mina's brain. She shuffled as if to get comfortable, the motion making Buck growl again. It was just enough of a distraction that she was able to slip closer to her purse.

"I didn't bring it. Someone put it in my bag."

It was Basheba's turn to look completely baffled. "You were holding it for a friend?"

"I didn't pack it. I only knew it was there just before we set out."

"You didn't get rid of it."

"I didn't see a reason to. It wasn't weighing me down."

The blonde was silent for a moment, too consumed by her thoughts to notice Mina's slowly creeping hand. The latch of her purse brushed her fingertips.

"All right," Basheba said, startling Mina and making her freeze. "Who put it in your bag?"

Mina's stomach dropped. "Why?"

"Why do you think?"

A fresh wave of ice replaced her blood. Mina's mother had always been gentle. A quiet, reserved, dignified kind of woman. She was the solid foundation Mina had built her identity upon. To hear she expected her daughter to kill had shaken everything she knew about herself, her mother, her world.

"I m not going to tell you that," Mina said, holding her gaze as she slipped her hand into her purse.

The motion went unnoticed.

"Why not?" Basheba asked pleasantly.

Mina saluted her with the mug, exaggerating the motion to keep the blonde's attention diverted. "Why do you think?" Mina glanced down to the muscular dog currently glaring at her. "I'm not going to let you kill my family."

"I have no plans to."

"Right."

"Honestly, I didn't even plan this. It's all in the spur of the moment. My brother used to call me impulsive."

Slivers of sorrow shattered the hard stone of Basheba's glare. The blonde dropped her gaze. A small motion that instantly drew Buck's concern. He stopped growling to nuzzle at Basheba's hand, receiving a smile and a scratch in return. It was barely a few seconds of distraction and Mina used them well, snatching her phone out of her bag and hitting the speed dial. Basheba sighed and rolled her eyes.

"Really? This will all be over before the police arrive, you know that, right? And my uncle, the good one, the dead one, taught me how to live pretty much off the grid. With Ozzie's funds, no one will find me."

The phone buzzed. "I'm not calling the police."

"Oh, Daddy Crane? I'm terrified," Basheba huffed.

"Not him," Mina said, internally praying for the call to connect before Basheba grew bored. "I'm calling the one person whose opinion you actually care about."

Understanding dawned on her face. Within seconds, she went from surprise, to annoyance, to childish guilt, like she had been found sneaking cookies before dinner.

"Mina, what a surprise."

Cadwyn's voice was calming. Smooth and deep. Like smoke and

honey. With a flurry of fingers, Mina switched the call to video chat and flipped the screen around. Forcing Basheba to look at the man who was, in all likelihood, her only friend.

"Basheba's trying to kill me."

"I'm sorry," Cadwyn said. "I think I misheard that."

Basheba opened her mouth, closed it, then slumped back against the side of the car, all the while glaring at Mina.

"You tattletale. See, now I really want to kill you."

Buck lurched forward, bracing his paws on the tow bar and snapping for Mina's leg. She retreated back as Cadwyn demanded to know what was happening and Basheba dismissed the whole thing. Heart in her throat, Mina knew she wasn't going to get a better time and blurted out over the commotion.

"I want to kill the Witch!"

Silence followed.

"Say that again," Cadwyn said slowly.

"You know she's already dead, right?" Basheba added.

Trying to summon some measure of dignity, Mina lifted her chin, carefully positioning the phone in an attempt to make sure they could all see each other.

"I want to go back. Now, in the Spring, when she won't be at the height of her powers. I want to end this."

Basheba shared a look with Cadwyn, both keeping their silence for a long time.

"Have you got any idea how to do that?" Basheba asked.

"Let me live and I'll tell you."

"You can always kill her later," Cadwyn said. "And, since this is something to be discussed in person, we can hang out for a bit."

Basheba pursed her lips in thought. "I still don't know if it'll be worth it."

"I'll pay for lunch," Cadwyn said.

"Deal."

Mina didn't know if she should feel blessed or insulted by such a low ransom but pushed on anyway. "Where would you like to meet?"

"Ozzie was just about to pick me up," Cadwyn said, a small smile playing on his wide lips. "We'll come to you."

CHAPTER 2

"I'm sorry about Emma," Ozzie said before glancing up from his phone. "Take this left."

They had to wait for a few kids to pass by on their bikes before they could set off down the road. The rental car hummed quietly over the narrow, well-tended streets. Wide sections of gravel bracketed the road, gradually giving way to long stretches of uninterrupted grass. Each of the houses had its space, with no fences or real driveways to speak of, and seemed to be hybrids of urban homes and rural ranch houses. Plain, comfortable, and oddly distinctive. The small town had a laid back, almost lazy feeling to it.

Ozzie checked the directions on his phone again before he added, "She's actually really nice."

"And a minor," Cadwyn said.

"I didn't know she was going to hit on you," Ozzie said. "Though, looking back, I probably should have. She's got this thing for motorbikes and older men. So, your entrance sealed the deal there."

"This whole conversation makes me very uncomfortable."

"Right. Sorry." He moved in his seat to face the older man. "You don't have to worry, though. She lost interest pretty quickly once I told her that you're a nurse."

Cadwyn looked at him from the corner of his eyes and bit back a smirk.

"No offense. I still think you're cool."

"I'm not offended at all."

Ozzie clicked his tongue and looked out the window. There wasn't much to draw his attention.

"Have you ever heard of cognac eyes?" Ozzie blurted. "Oh, straight through this stop sign."

Cadwyn slowed, carefully checking the deserted street twice before continuing on.

"Once or twice. Why?"

"Emma got prissy about it. Insisted your eyes are *cognac*." Ozzie puffed out a breath. "They're brown. She sounds so pretentious sometimes."

"And I'm uncomfortable again," Cadwyn said before pressing his wide mouth into a thin line.

"Change the subject?"

"Please." Before Ozzie could think up another topic, Cadwyn picked one. "I didn't know they let fifteen-year-olds have pilot licenses."

"I'm sixteen now, remember?"

"Right. Sorry."

"Anyway, you can begin flight training at any age. Now that I'm *sixteen*," he said, exaggerating the word until Cadwyn chuckled, "I can fly solo. I won't be eligible for a private pilot certificate until next year, though."

"You weren't flying solo. You had your instructor," Cadwyn hid his cringe to add, "and some passengers."

Ozzie shrugged sheepishly. "Dallas to Massachusetts is a long flight and my friends wanted to keep me company. They've all had Spring Break in Texas before and got bored."

"I understand." Of course, he had no idea. Cadwyn wasn't a Sewall or a Davis. He had no idea what it was like to be insanely, almost insultingly, rich. It just seemed like the thing to say.

"And when they heard I was coming to pick you up—"

"Wait. They were interested in meeting me? What have you told them?"

Ozzie nodded once as if that answered Cadwyn's question and continued on. "Anyway, it was good we had Kai tagging along, now that we've changed our plans and are staying here. Her family has a plane here in New Jersey, so they won't all have to fly commercial to New York."

"I'm glad we could help them escape such a horror," Cadwyn chuckled.

"Emma's allergic to public transportation," Ozzie replied.

"That's not a thing."

"She says she breaks out in hives."

Cadwyn's laughter grew. "As a medical professional, I'm telling you, that's not how allergies work."

"Oh. So, I've just been flying her around for nothing?" He deflated slightly. "Yeah, that figures."

"How long have you been flying?" Cadwyn asked, his voice warm and comforting, easing Ozzie's wounded pride.

"We've always had a private jet." Looking purposefully out of the window, he quickly added, "But I only started taking lessons in November."

"After the Harvest."

Ozzie cringed. There was no reason for him to be embarrassed, he knew that. He just hated the fact that he seemed to be the only one affected by their time in the Witch Woods. Cadwyn had gone right back to working with the criminally insane, casually dealing with serial killers and cannibals. The girls had picked a wooded, rural area to meet up. Ozzie broke out in a cold sweat just going into his backyard now, and that was just a few yards of trees to give the deer something to wander through. When he chanced a glance at the older man, he found Cadwyn was grinning, his teeth straight and perfect.

"You're laughing at me?"

"What? No, of course not. I'm proud of you."

"Huh?"

"It's easy to wallow in your own pain. Believe me, I know. But you decided to improve yourself." Deep lines fanned out from the corner of Cadwyn's eyes as he looked at Ozzie again. "That takes a lot of strength. I'm impressed."

"Oh." Fire prickled Ozzie's cheeks. "Full disclosure, I don't know how to respond to that."

"You don't have to say anything."

"I'm uncomfortable," Ozzie teased.

"You didn't have a minor hitting on you for an hour!"

Cadwyn looked so dramatically traumatized that Ozzie couldn't help but burst into laughter.

"At least she's pretty."

"I'm in my thirties!"

"When you say it like that, you do sound like a creep."

"I didn't do anything," he protested.

Ozzie laughed harder. No matter what the Witch had thrown at them, Cadwyn had always been calm and serene. A man in complete control of himself and his emotions. Ozzie was honor-bound to mercilessly exploit this sudden weakness.

They ended up talking over each other, their rapid-fire words bleeding into each other, and almost missed the diner. With a slight curse and a sharp turn on the wheel, Cadwyn cut across the gravel road and lurched into a parking place. He cut the engine and turned fully to Ozzie.

"Do *not* tell your mother I did that."

"She's going to swear at you a lot," Ozzie grinned. "But it'll all be in Korean, so you won't understand most of it anyway."

"That doesn't make it better."

Out of the car, with the sun shining brightly over the treetops and the scent of fries in the air, Ozzie finally felt brave enough to ask.

"Did Basheba really try to kill Mina?"

"Yeah. But she's over that now. Don't worry about it."

Ozzie's thick eyebrows jumped to his hairline. Always observant, Cadwyn paused midstride and sighed.

"They had an issue between the two of them. It's handled now."

"Does she always try to kill people?"

"Not always," Cadwyn shrugged.

"How is this not freaking you out?"

Rounding the front of the car, Cadwyn gently placed his large hand on Ozzie's shoulder, careful to avoid the newly healed break.

"Basheba's lived with the Witch longer than any of us. That affects you."

"You're older," Ozzie noted.

"I've only been selected once," Cadwyn said. "The Witch singled her out twice. And she's been in more search parties than anyone else alive. That much time in the Witch Woods does things to you."

"So, we let her try and kill people?"

Cadwyn's lips moved soundlessly, but his eyes remained sure.

He'd let her, Ozzie thought.

"You wouldn't do something like that. And a demon tortured you for months." Ozzie regretted the words as soon as they left his mouth. The moment he saw Cadwyn flinch. *Good going, Ozzie. Bring up the demon that killed his brother.*

"I've never known her to do anything without provocation," Cadwyn said smoothly.

"What about her uncle? She slashed his face because he touched her hair."

"That's just what you observed. We don't know what was going on between them." Cadwyn continued before Ozzie could say anything else. "Whatever happened between the girls, it's done. No good will come from you opening that wound. Understand?"

"Yeah."

Ozzie's recent growth spurt still couldn't compete with Cadwyn's lofty six feet. The older man ducked his head until he could catch Ozzie's downcast gaze.

"She's not going to hurt you."

"She might hurt other people, though."

He hesitated, clearly choosing his words in his head before letting them slip past his lips.

"Basheba has survived this long because she doesn't let threats to her safety go unpunished. The Cranes know that. They knew the consequences of their actions, and decided to threaten her anyway. I'm not saying I think Mina should carry the blame for it. I don't. I told Basheba. She listened. And she agrees with me."

"But—"

"It's done, Ozzie. Don't bring it up."

He nodded numbly and followed the towering man to the diner door. Cadwyn opened the fly screen, holding it a while to let Ozzie enter first. Shadows lingered in the old box-like structure. Preoccupied with his thoughts, Ozzie didn't notice the creature until it was looming over him. It had large, unblinking eyes and fangs longer than his hand. Its big, leathery wings were stretched wide to blot out the overhead lights. A startled cry ripped from his lungs as he staggered away. He slammed into Cadwyn's chest and his sneakers slipped over the polished wood floor. If the older man hadn't gripped him by the shoulders, he would have fallen to the ground. A frantic heartbeat passed, and Ozzie realized the creature wasn't coming for him.

"It's a statue," he mumbled, heat pulsating against his cheeks.

"I'd say it's taxidermy," Cadwyn said.

"What animal?"

Cadwyn hummed thoughtfully. "Well, those legs are obviously from a horse. And maybe a Doberman's head, though the muzzle is too wide. The claws look bird-like. Ostrich, maybe? I have no idea where they got the wings from."

Hearing Cadwyn verbally dissect the monster made Ozzie feel steadier. Which, in turn, left him feeling like a moron for shrieking like that in a public place. Sheepishly, he glanced around. The person behind the counter was laughing at him, and there was a man in a distant booth who seemed just as amused. Thankfully, the place was otherwise deserted. The back doors opened up to a grassy patch speckled with picnic tables. It gave him a clear view of Mina jogging toward them.

Only two years separated them. It was hardly anything. But he always felt like a little kid around her. She was just so put together. Sophisticated, or stylish, or something he couldn't put his finger on. It made it harder to ignore the fact that she was gorgeous. Huge ebony eyes, tawny skin, hair with that loose curl thing that some of his friends spent hours at the salon to get. *How can someone who's just been poisoned look so pretty?* He remembered not to stare just as she passed the threshold.

"Hey, guys," she beamed. "I am so glad you're here. I hope it wasn't too out of your way."

"Don't worry about it," Cadwyn said as he slipped around Ozzie to greet her.

They shared a quick hug before he slipped a penlight out of his back pocket and clicked it on. "How are you?"

With a nod, Mina casually rattled off the symptoms. "I had a slight fever that broke about an hour ago. Still suffering a bit of dry mouth. Sweating and increased heart rate are starting to even out."

First, she looked at the penlight he shone in her eyes, then lifted her gaze to the ceiling when instructed.

"What's your name?"

"Willimina Crane."

"And his?" He jerked one thumb toward Ozzie while he checked her pulse.

"Osgood Sewall. I mean, Davis. Sorry. Hi, by the way."

"Hey," Ozzie said with an awkward wave he quickly regretted. "And either way's fine."

Cadwyn's expression remained carefully neutral as he surveyed the girl. "Where are you?"

"Devil's Diner in New Jersey."

"And why are we here?"

"It's where Basheba Bell chose for our meeting place."

"Oh, no. That wasn't one of the health check questions," Cadwyn said with a smile. "I just don't get why she picked here."

The squint of Mina's eyes made it clear she knew Cadwyn was just trying to break the tension.

"Apparently, there've been sightings of the New Jersey Devil in the woods out back. She's hoping she'll catch a glimpse before we go."

"The things that girl gets up to," Cadwyn mumbled, more amused than frustrated. Straightening, he clicked off his light. "How much did you drink?"

"Just a sip."

"Any hallucinations?"

"No."

"Still peeing?"

"Cadwyn," Ozzie whispered sharply.

Cadwyn looked confused for a second, as if he didn't see how asking a girl that question in public was strange.

"Inability to urinate is a sign of Belladonna poisoning." Turning his full attention back to Mina, he added, "But you don't have to answer. I was just doing my due diligence. All the evidence suggests you're fine."

"Are you sure?" Mina asked.

"You're not flushed. No memory loss. You're not slurring your speech, or having seizures." He listed off. "I'm guessing you didn't ingest anywhere near enough to be worried."

"Isn't any dose deadly?" Ozzie asked.

Cadwyn laughed until he realized that he was serious. "No. It's used a lot in medicine. For a young woman in otherwise good health, the amount she took shouldn't be a problem."

"Good thing I called you, then," Mina sighed in relief.

"Nah, you would have talked her around."

"You grossly overestimate how much affection she has for me," Mina dismissed as she turned. "Come on. She's out this way."

Cadwyn caught her arm. A gentle touch that forced her to pause all the same.

"You think Basheba changed her mind because we're friends?" he asked with all seriousness.

"Of course. What else am I supposed to think?"

A frown curved his lips, his brow furrowed, and his eyes clouded with something Ozzie couldn't define.

"I'm going to give you the same advice I gave her when she was your age," he said at last.

Mina snuck a quick glance at Ozzie. "Okay."

"Anyone who says, 'if you love me, you'll do this,' doesn't love you. They're trying to emotionally manipulate you."

Mina pulled her arm free of his grip. "I don't get where this is coming from. But, sometimes, people say that because they know what's best for you. Sometimes, you have to do things you don't want to for the people you care about."

"Caring about someone demands you respect them enough to listen to them. Truly listen and think about what they tell you. It doesn't necessitate obedience. Anyone who tells you that it does isn't thinking about what's best for you. They're thinking about themselves."

The muscles around Mina's eyes pinched tight. She bit her lips like she was trying to keep her response to herself. But the moment passed quickly, and she soon pulled herself to full height, hiding her discomfort behind a smile.

"I'll keep it in mind. Thank you. Any other words of wisdom?"

There was a sharp edge in the last sentence that Cadwyn deliberately ignored. "Never trust someone when they tell you their spouse 'just doesn't understand them.' My Grandma told me that one."

Mina blinked. "Was that ever useful to you?"

"My first boss said that to me word for word, actually."

"Right." Her mouth hung open as her brow furrowed. "Right. Well, come on."

Ozzie waited until Mina was a few steps ahead before he whispered to Cadwyn, "You told Basheba that?"

Cadwyn nodded.

He chuckled. "I wouldn't think she'd need to hear it."

"I know it's a radical concept, Ozzie, but she is human. Just like the rest of us."

CHAPTER 3

Buck almost barreled Mina over as he rushed past her, making a beeline for Cadwyn. It was hard to tell which one of them was more excited at being reunited. Cadwyn dropped to one knee to let the colossal dog balance his two front paws on his shoulders. A nice gesture that left them both toppling onto the grass. The more Cadwyn laughed, the more Buck attacked with licks and yelps.

"I missed you, too, buddy," Cadwyn said between gasps.

Seemingly satisfied by that, Buck turned his attention to Ozzie, who was a little more apprehensive. Eventually, once both boys were covered in a layer of slobber, the Rottweiler turned and bounded back to the far picnic table. There was barely enough room for him underneath, but he crammed himself in there anyway. Basheba kicked off her shoes to rub her bare feet against his side. The table rattled as Buck tried to roll in the confined space. Through sheer determination, he ended up on his back so Basheba could absently rub his belly. All the while, the blonde stared at the woods. She only acknowledged the group at all when Cadwyn slipped onto the seat opposite her. Between the table's lack of room and Buck's presence, he opted for keeping his legs in the open.

"Hey," he smiled.

By now, Mina had been around Basheba for half of the day. This was the first time the blonde flashed a real smile.

"Hey, you made it. I got a gift for you."

"Is it being exposed to your sparkling personality?" Cadwyn teased.

Basheba was already searching through the backpack she kept with her almost all of the time.

"Nah, I'm horrible."

"I'll take your dog," Cadwyn offered.

"I will literally stab you."

Cadwyn brushed off the threat with a one-shoulder shrug. "Sounds about right."

Mina and Ozzie joined them just as Basheba leaned across the table and yanked a huge, fluffy, wolf head beanie over his dark blonde hair. Flaps that ended in pompoms flopped over Cadwyn's ears to brush against his collar bones.

"Perfect," Basheba said.

Cadwyn bit back a smile. "I have questions."

"I went to a wolf reserve," she said, looking somewhat smug at her gift. "Feel free to eat it."

"Are you still going on about those pretzels?" Cadwyn asked. "That was one time."

"They were *alien* pretzels. You can't get them just anywhere."

"You abandoned them."

"It was still my food, Cad," she hissed.

He pulled the beanie off of his head so he could study it. "You have to let it go."

"There's no statute of limitations on food theft!"

The flash of anger and the accusatory jab of her finger only made Cadwyn burst into laughter. *Does he honestly have no fear of her?* Mina wondered. *Or does he think she'll never turn on him?*

The thoughts were a welcome relief from what had been cluttering her head. Cadwyn's passing words had burrowed into her mind like woodworms. Conjuring up all the thousands of memories of all the times her family had repeated almost that exact configuration of words against her.

You're our daughter. We love you. You'll do this for us, right?

Sucking in a deep breath, she pushed the thoughts aside and rested her hands on the table.

"Can we get this meeting started?"

"I can't listen to you without food," Basheba said before she made purposeful eye contact with Cadwyn. "As I was promised."

"Yeah, yeah."

"I'm hungry."

"I'm going," he shot back. "Don't sink your teeth into my leg just yet."

Basheba scoffed, "But you have such good thighs."

After a long moment, Cadwyn asked with muted seriousness. "Should I be flattered or disturbed?"

"Depends how long you take to bring me my food."

"Right," he straightened and swept a hand around the table. "Burgers all round?"

While Cadwyn jogged back to the building to place the orders, Ozzie took a seat next to Basheba. The tension in the teenager's shoulders quickly melted away as they caught each other up about their injuries and the legend of the Jersey Devil. By the time she presented him with his own gift, Ozzie was all smiles and laughter. The fuzzy blue plushie only made him laugh harder.

"An octopus," he chuckled. "Which aquarium did you go to?"

"That's a replica of the dreaded kraken of Thunderbird Lake, you uneducated plebian."

"Yeah, definitely too cashed up to be a plebian, but roll on," Ozzie grinned.

Watching Basheba laugh and smile, it was hard to believe what had happened only a few hours ago. *She's a good liar,* Mina thought, recalling the police officer in Black River. Basheba had managed to convince him she was a child so she could get away with a lot more. It would have been impressive if it wasn't so insidious.

Finally, Cadwyn returned with a handful of cups and a jug of pop. He poured a glass for everyone and handed Mina hers. It was a small, wordless gesture that carried a world of reassurance. *This is safe to drink.*

"Thank you," Mina said, clutching the cup protectively to her stomach. "Does anyone mind if I get started now? While we're waiting?"

"I'm interested," Ozzie chirped while Cadwyn plucked the plushie out of his hands to better examine it.

"Do I have time for a cigarette?" Cadwyn asked absently.

The question drew Basheba's attention. "I thought you only smoked in October?"

Cadwyn scrunched his mouth up. "It's like Pavlovian Conditioning. Going into Black River? Put some tar in your lungs."

Basheba absently sipped at her drink. "Just throwing it out there, but I'm not a huge fan of the smell. Do you mind sitting downwind?"

"I just got comfortable." He drummed his fingers on the table as he thought it over. "It's too much trouble. I just won't. Okay, Mina. You have my full attention."

Mina had watched the interaction carefully, studying their dynamics. Her normal approach to befriending the blonde hadn't worked all that well. So, Mina had decided to fall back on what she knew—the scientific method. *Observation. Hypothesis. Experimentation.* Cadwyn was the only person Mina had seen Basheba interreact with in a solely positive way. It now seemed that understanding why, and successfully emulating that relationship, was important for her survival.

"Mina?" Ozzie asked.

"Right." Mina drew in a deep breath and pulled her bag out from under the table.

Buck didn't so much as lift his head. Resting it on the edge of the table, she opened it and pulled out a handful of books and maps.

"I want to kill the Witch," Mina said.

"I love the enthusiasm," Basheba said. "I just don't fully understand how you plan to do that."

Ozzie looked around the table. "Can you even kill a ghost. Like, is it possible?"

"Kill might not be the best word," Mina said as she placed the books and papers on the table, and stowed away her bag again. "But it achieves the same thing. I want to cut her off from this world and send her to whatever comes after it."

"Again, I ask *how*." Basheba played with the beading condensation on her glass with one fingertip. "I'm sure you've heard all the stories about people trying to do just what you're suggesting. None of those stories have a happy ending."

"I know. I've done my research." Mina placed her hand on the small mountain of notebooks. "I found out it's been over half a century since someone last tried. There's been a lot of advances since then. And, between us, we have two distinct advantages that none of the other groups had."

"If she says, 'friendship and a can-do attitude,' I'm going to try and kill her again," Basheba whispered to Cadwyn.

Her tone was light and teasing, but there was iron underneath; something that promised that she wasn't joking.

Mina cleared her throat. "I meant you and Cadwyn."

The two people in question shared a mutually confused glance before Cadwyn ventured.

"I'm not sure I follow."

"Well." Mina had practiced the speech to perfection, but now couldn't remember how it started. "My family keeps records. Diaries. I looked into them all, and then found what I could about the other members of the, for lack of better phrasing, Witch-hunting groups. Those who survived continued their diaries and, after reading a few of them, it became clear they lacked enough knowledge to be prepared."

Cadwyn drew in a deep breath as if steadying himself. "And I've lived with a demon."

While his face remained calm, Mina knew she had to tread carefully. "What happened with your brother was horrible, and I don't want to bring up bad memories. But the experience would have offered a different kind of education. You know how they think, what to expect, and it's left you rather unflappable."

Cadwyn only stared at her. Just when she was sure she had lost and offended him, he ran his hand roughly through his hair, bringing his bangs into disarray.

"Well, you've got me there."

Now came the harder part. Meeting Basheba's eyes, Mina reminded herself to keep to the facts.

"You're the only person alive who the Witch has selected twice."

"I'm starting to think Katrina has a crush on me," Basheba dismissed, although it was clear she had no small measure of pride over her survival rate.

"And you've been to the woods more times than that," Mina continued, hoping to take advantage of her good mood.

"A few times," Basheba confirmed.

Ozzie snapped around to face her. "Wait. You have? Why?"

"It's tradition. We create search parties to go on and find the bodies of those who didn't make it out. All the families pitch in."

"How old were you when you...? The first time, I mean."

"Five or so. I don't really remember."

Ozzie looked horrified. "What? Why would anyone do that?"

"Because I'm a Bell," she cut in, fire crackling along the edges of her words. A small warning that he was getting far too close to insulting her family. "That always comes with a certain degree of guilt. If Griogair Bell had just given her the property back, given her a cut of his proceeds, bent to the irrational demands of a vile woman, all of this wouldn't have happened. Making sure the murdered get a decent burial is the least we can do." Within the space of a second, she was all smiles while she brought the glass to her lips. "Isn't that the stupidest thing you've ever heard? Talk about victim blaming."

"So, they took you to find dead bodies?" Ozzie asked, still not satisfied.

"Dad used to bring me around the edges of the woods, show me the weird creatures Katrina had created," Basheba said, a nostalgic warmth filling her gaze. "He was so proud I was never afraid."

"Never?" Ozzie asked softly.

"He had these big hands, my dad," Basheba whispered, more to herself than anyone else. "When he held my hand, I couldn't even see my fingers. I thought he was a giant."

The moment shattered and Basheba snapped her head up. She almost looked stunned that she had said any of it aloud. Snatching up her glass, she mumbled something about being hungry before draining and refilling her cup. No one knew what to say, not until Cadwyn broke the silence.

"Your dad was five-five."

She smacked her glass down. "I was really little at the time. He seemed bigger."

"Yeah," Cadwyn grinned, tipping his glass toward her. "Larger than life."

"From womb to tomb," Basheba recited and clinked her glass against his.

While Mina didn't understand the reference, she knew well enough not to ask. Basheba had only mentioned her father a few times. But each time, it was with adoration and raw love. It was clear she had idolized the man. Mina had come to suspect that Basheba was more volatile with love than with hate. She wasn't going to even approach the topic until she knew she was on firm ground.

"You know Katrina," Mina ventured. "At the very least, you obviously tick her off. So, between the two of you, we have more knowledge than any of the other groups that have gone before us."

"And what do you bring to the table?" Basheba asked.

"Relentless determination."

"Yet everyone calls me stubborn as an insult," Basheba muttered.

"How about history, then? The Cranes are the largest surviving family of the four. We keep records. I can tell you the tricks the Witch has used in the past. The assault methods that failed—"

"Have you ever been to Black River outside of the Harvest season?" Basheba cut in.

"Well," she stammered. "No."

28

"It's not just Katrina you have to worry about. It's the cult."

"There's a cult now?" Ozzie asked.

Cadwyn caught the teenager's eyes. "That's how Basheba addresses the locals."

"I address them like that because they're a dang cult," she snapped. "Or at least a percentage of them are."

Ozzie tipped his head in question. "What percentage?"

"Forty-three," Basheba answered without hesitation.

Cadwyn almost choked on his drink. "Show me the math."

"What is your obsession with math and evidence?" Basheba accused.

"What do you mean by 'cult'? No one told me about that," Ozzie cut in.

Feeling she was quickly losing control of the conversation, Mina rushed to assure him. "There's no cult. It's just Basheba's theory that the townsfolk are working with the Witch."

His face scrunched up. "Why would anyone do that?"

"Because their entire livelihood depends on her," Basheba dismissed. "And it doesn't matter if you believe me or not. All of you have bigger things to worry about."

"Oh no. Now what?" Ozzie said.

"My uncle owns Witch's Brew. You know, that café we all meet at each year? If we enter town, he'll eventually find out, and then the phone calls will begin, and the Kings will descend."

"Kings?" Ozzie asked.

"Oh, right, you're new." Basheba drew in a deep breath. "Being haunted by a dead witch makes people close ranks and cling to what they know. A fascinating trend that happened to each one of the four families is that they became kind of a monarchy. A very patriarchal, power restrictive monarchy. They call the shots, and they don't like anyone going to town without their knowledge or permission. Because heaven forbid we aggravate our personal serial killer."

"That's not true." Mina rolled her eyes.

"My cousin Jeffery is the Winthrop family leader," Cadwyn said.

Basheba snapped her fingers and pointed to him. "That's what they call it to soften the blow."

"I've heard Percival call his brother 'family leader,'" Ozzie said with a frown.

"Zachariah Sewall," Basheba nodded. "King of the Sewall line."

Ozzie turned to Mina. "Who's your family's king?"

"We just listen to our elders. As is respectful."

"Her daddy," Basheba chirped. "Mina, our little princess."

A flash of anger twisted up Mina's mouth. "So your uncle is your king? He's the only man left."

Basheba laughed outright and reached across the table. Mina flinched back before she realized the blonde was only going for the map.

Spreading the map of Black River out before her, she explained, "Pregnancy is a horror show I will have no part in. And my uncle would never let his precious virginial daughter be sullied by the touch of a man. Which works out pretty well, because she's incredibly gay. There's no one left."

"What about your uncle?" Mina cut in. "He still capable of having children?"

"I live in dread of the day he realizes he can be a sperm donor," Basheba admitted. "Luckily, the only woman who could tolerate him left him decades ago. He's not popping out any more kids. Our line is dead. Can't really be a king if you have no subjects."

"That's one way of looking at it," Cadwyn said into his glass.

Basheba quirked an eyebrow. For once, Cadwyn hesitated.

"Jeffery thinks—and I can't stress enough that this is *his* opinion, not mine—that if you refuse to acknowledge Isaac as your leader, then the remaining Bells should be brought into the Winthrop family."

"Does he now?" Like snow melting in the Spring, every trace of emotion melted from Basheba's face. "'Brought in' meaning I'd be under Jeffery Winthrop's control?"

"Well," Cadwyn cleared his throat. "Ah, there would be an

expectation that you would turn to him and the other Winthrop elders for advice. Yes."

"Just advice? Or that I'd follow through on his orders?"

Cadwyn was too busy drinking to reply.

"So, by your cousin's thinking, if I refuse to bow to my blood relative, I should bow to him, instead?" The muscles in her jaw twitched. "Isn't that interesting."

"You've made a reputation for yourself, Basheba," Cadwyn tried to soothe. "I got the impression that all of the families want control over you."

"Control," she repeated.

"I'm sure that's just a bad choice of words," Ozzie cut in with a nervous laugh.

"Don't bother, Ozzie," Basheba said. "I've known for years they don't see me as an equal."

"I'm sure that's not true," Mina said.

"No, it is." The smile the blonde gave was sharp and full of venom. "Every one of them is beneath me. Mom taught me that well enough."

Sensing the dangers of any follow-up questions, Cadwyn cut in before the others to stress, "I want it stated for the record that I don't agree with Jeffery's plan or thought process."

Basheba nodded, her gaze unfixed. "The record acknowledges the protests of Cadwyn Winthrop."

Cadwyn licked his lips. "He's just worried your coup will spread."

A burst of laughter passed her lips. "My coup?"

"Well, you are rebelling against your rightful king," Cadwyn said, refreshing Basheba's glass as if he wanted to distract her.

Basheba hummed, her gaze turning dreamy. "I would look good in a crown. But then I'd have the world's stupidest subjects. Doesn't seem worth it."

"Would they really try to stop us?" Ozzie asked.

"You're not coming," Cadwyn said.

Ozzie bristled. "Why not?"

"You're *sixteen*," Cadwyn replied.

"I went into the woods when I was fifteen."

"We didn't have a choice, then. We do now."

"Shouldn't I have that choice?"

"You're a minor," Cadwyn said. "You can't even vote yet."

"We need him," Mina said. It was a little unnerving to suddenly have their undivided attention. "At least, we need his credit card."

"Explain," Cadwyn snapped.

"Well, I thought we'd get a hotel room to serve as our base of operations before heading out. Making sure we're well-rested and such."

"What's your point?" Cadwyn asked.

"You need to present identification to book a room. If Basheba's right, we're working against ourselves to use our well-known names. Everyone there knows Sewall. No one knows Davis."

"You know what?" Basheba suddenly declared. "I've got nothing else to do this weekend. I'll join your suicide mission."

"Me too," Ozzie declared before Cadwyn could respond.

He glared at the teen and Basheba in turn. Ozzie avoided the gaze but Basheba just smiled.

"Couldn't just back me up?" he asked her.

Basheba giggled, leaning back as the food arrived. "Vive la Révolution."

Chapter 4

Apple blossoms coated the apple trees white. Pristine petals drifted over the rural road like snow, twisting in the air and gathering in the lush grass. The vibrant oranges and reds of the Fall seasons had been replaced with an explosion of green. A blanket of wildflowers covered the rolling hills, pushed back only by the small farms of the same vibrance. Morning light cut through the thick foliage to flash against Basheba's aviator sunglasses. The crisp morning air churned in through the driver's side window as she drove, toying at her hair and carrying the scents of the countryside into her car.

The thirteen-hour drive had proven too much for the others and, one by one, they had each fallen asleep. Mina and Ozzie shared the mattress that filled the trunk and back seat, with Buck happily snuggled between them. Cadwyn sat in the front passenger seat, his head propped up on the window and generally too big for the space. He had taken the wheel until they stopped for dinner the night before. She had protested at first, but he had stood firm, insisting she needed some time to sleep and that he could easily drive while she dozed.

Like I haven't driven way farther on less sleep before.

It hadn't taken long for the others to pick his side, refusing to be in a car with such a 'fatigued' driver. Basheba had caved when Ozzie started offering to buy their flights. Leaving her car behind was a far worse option than letting Cadwyn drive it for a few hours. And they all refused to leave without her.

Knowing she was defeated, and that they might have a point in regard to road safety, didn't make the reality any easier to accept. It had only been for a few hours but the damage was done. Even now, hours after she had regained control of the driver's seat, she felt the shift. It was different now. The gentle rumble of her parent's car sounded the same. The sense of freedom and safety she had always felt within its metal body was still there. But it was different now. It all felt further away. *He* felt further away.

Her father hadn't had much to leave her when he died. There was the car, though. And she had the knowledge that she had been the only one to drive it since his death. She had been the only one to sit where he had sat. To touch the stick shift and wheel. Her feet had pressed the pedals and it felt like she was following in his footsteps. For two years she'd had that. A silly, sentimental little thought to keep her connected to the dead. Now, Cadwyn had been in the driver's seat and that link was severed. Never to be fixed again. The tradition was over. *What do I have left?*

Taking one hand from the steering wheel, she pulled at the twine looped around her neck. A few tugs and the numerous wedding rings slipped free of her shirt. They clattered against each other and against the single locket that dangled from the middle of the group.

They were the only true mementos she had of the dead, and she guarded them with savage ferocity. The few photographs she had were incomplete. There was always someone missing. Her uncle had taken everything else. In the beginning, no one had been bothered. It had been easier to leave one person in charge of dividing up the estates since any legitimate will would demand a death certificate. Lawyers would ask too many questions. Isaac had his own business. No one else wanted to waste their limited lifespans on paperwork. He was setting up high-interest trust funds, growing what little they had to supply for the next generation. It was her mother who had started the tradition of keeping the rings.

A small smile crept across Basheba's lips as she recalled the first time she had come back from a body retrieval to find her uncle waiting for her. He had crouched down before her, one hand stroking her hair as he asked if she had found her great-grandmother's engagement ring.

Basheba had nodded, and her uncle's smile had spread.

"What a good girl you are," he had said, patting her hair with renewed strength. "Hand it over."

Basheba's gloved fingers hadn't been quick enough to fish it out of her pocket before Basheba's mother had swooped down upon them, shoving Isaac into the dirt. It was as if Isaac always forgot the Bells, including himself, weren't all that physically imposing. Their family tended to be small, fragile, and about as visually intimidating as a newborn fawn. At six-foot-three, Basheba's mother had towered over him, no matter how he puffed himself up. But that day, in that moment, was the first time Basheba had seen Isaac for what he really was—a scared little man cowering in her mother's shadow.

"Baba, keep the ring in your pocket, okay?" Her mother had instructed.

Basheba almost teared up at the memory. It had been over two years since anyone had used her nickname.

"Gwen, be reasonable," her uncle snarled from her memory. "She's a child. She'll lose it."

"She managed to bring it out of the Witch Woods just fine."

Isaac's voice had turned into a whisper. "It's worth ten thousand dollars."

It was the first time Basheba had ever heard her mother cuss someone out. She hadn't understood most of the words at the time, but now they made her laugh.

"I knew you've been selling them, you son of—"

"I have them appraised," Isaac had insisted. "That's the intelligent thing to do."

"Where are the—"

"You can't think Basheba is responsible enough. She'll lose it."

When she next spoke, it had been with an icy calm. "Interrupt me again. I dare you."

Isaac had slinked off into the safety of the grieving crowd, leaving Basheba to be scooped up into her mother's arms. No one had ever had hair as soft as her mother's. It had been the perfect place to hide her face when she cried.

"Shh, little lamb. You didn't do anything wrong." Her mother's eyes had sparkled when she smiled at her. "I want you to keep the rings, keep them safe until I ask for them, okay? Can you do that?"

"Daddy told me to give them to Uncle Isaac."

"Daddy doesn't always know what's best."

The tip of Basheba's nose tingled with the memory of her mother tapping a finger against it. Still smiling, she baaed like a sheep, coaxing Basheba to return the gesture until they were both giggling.

A stray beam of light slipped under Basheba's sunglasses and struck her eyes, making her flinch, severing the memory. She released the rings long enough to wipe a stray tear away. Unthinkingly, her hand drifted back, this time finding her great-grandmother's ruby ring. *I wonder if uncle knows I still have them.* The notion that he did made her smile again. A sharp intake of breath made her jump and she snapped around.

"What are you thinking about?" Cadwyn asked with a yawn.

She shoved the cluster of rings into her top. "Nothing."

Lines creased his forehead as his eyes tracked the movement.

"What are you looking at?" The words came out as a snarl, fueled by her irrational fear that sharing any of her memories would somehow make her forget.

"Nothing," he said cautiously.

"Oh? Nothing? Really?"

His gaze flicked between her shirt and her eyes, clearly searching for a way to extract himself from the situation.

"I'm just inappropriately staring at your chest," he offered.

Basheba bit the inside of her cheek to keep from smiling. Watching his face turn red as he held back his laughter made her crack. Their chuckling made the others stir and they were all awake as she took the turn, leaving behind the main road and cutting through the flower drenched fields. Mina and Ozzie spent most of the remaining drive checking in with their parents, both blatantly lying about where they were. Ozzie was in New York with his friends, who were apparently confirming the lie on their end. Mina, on the other hand, was in Cambridge, taking a Harvard campus tour with her friends.

"Okay, dad. I've got to go, one of the lectures is starting." Mina caught Basheba's amused gaze in the review mirror and twisted slightly, seeking the privacy that she couldn't possibly achieve. "Okay. Love you, too. Bye." She hung up and sighed. "Okay, let's hear it."

"I've got a Harvard jersey in the bag back there if you want it. Help sell the lie."

"Why would you have a Harvard jersey?"

Basheba forced herself not to look back at her. "I got it when I went there."

Mina jolted as if she had been struck with a cattle prod. "You went to Harvard?"

"The tours are open to the public," Cadwyn cut in. "Don't tease her, Basheba."

"Don't judge my hobbies," she shot back.

"For the record, as a responsible adult, I'm not on board with everyone lying to their parental units," Cadwyn said, speaking loud enough for everyone in the car to hear.

Basheba watched him out of the corner of her eyes. "Are you going to do anything about it?"

"And have you call me a tattletale?" he asked, aghast. "I'd never survive that kind of emotional assault."

Basheba's reply lodged in her throat as she made the final turn and entered the apple orchard. It was something beyond words or sensation. Something bone-deep. As they traveled down the narrow gravel road, the gnarled limbs of the tree arching above them like clutching fingers, their clustered flowers blotting out the sun, a little voice deep inside her soul whispered the truth. *We're home.*

Silence took the car as they traveled the last few miles, surrounded by the perfect rows of trees, each brimming with too much life to see far beyond them. Barely anyone worked the fields. Mostly, it was just younger kids who had clearly been roped into helping their relatives over the school break. One or two looked up at the passing car, but most just went about their work erecting scarecrows.

"We should pick a different spot," Basheba said, her voice barely rising over the hum of the old car's engine.

"This is the only place that met all of your demands," Mina huffed. "A bed and breakfast on the outskirts of town. Few rooms, with minimal bookings. Easy access to the highway with no environmental barriers to hinder escape. It took me ages to find this place."

"They're putting scarecrows up in an apple orchard," Basheba said. "Clearly, they've signed up for Team Katrina."

"Apple orchards don't use scarecrows?" Ozzie asked, reaching into the front seat to nudge Cadwyn's shoulder.

"I don't know anything about farming."

"Their website used the term 'rustic aesthetic' so much it's lost all meaning to me," Mina said. "It could just be decoration."

"When are you guys going to learn that I'm never wrong about these things?" Basheba demanded.

"Okay, say you're right, where do you suggest we go?" Mina might have kept her tone rational and pleasant, but Basheba knew the girl was luring her into a trap. "Any neighboring town is going to take hours out of our day just getting back and forth. All the other places are closer to main street Black River and don't take dogs. Our only other option is camping out, and I'm not good with that."

"I'm not either," Cadwyn chimed in. "I'd prefer a sturdy door I can lock."

Basheba drew in a long, deep breath, trying to buy herself some time to think. But they had long since exhausted their options before the previous day's dinner. *There's nowhere safe for us in Black River,* she thought. She gripped the wheel to keep from seeking out her parent's wedding rings again.

"All right," she said at last. "But I retain the right to tell everyone 'I told you so.'"

Cadwyn caught Mina's gaze over the back of his seat. "That's as good as you're going to get. Take the win."

"All right," Mina said, somewhat bitterly.

It made Basheba smile. But that soon faded when the apple flowers parted just enough to bring the two-story farmhouse into view. Its baby blue siding blended harmoniously with the meticulously tended garden surrounding it. The bushes hung heavy with blooming flowers and the open yard was a field of lush grass.

"I hate to say it. But this looks nice. Like something out of a fairytale," Ozzie said.

"Appropriate, given the wicked witch lurking about," Mina mumbled.

They kept quiet as Basheba slowed the car and inched up the last of the driveway. Someone came out onto the front porch as they approached. She waved them closer, a warm and sunny grin on her face.

"Who's that?" Ozzie asked.

"The owner, I suppose," Mina said.

"Huh," Ozzie said. "Not gonna lie, I was expecting more of a grandmother archetype."

The woman's lipstick matched her blazing red hair and 50's era dress. It was hard to tell her age but she looked to be younger than Cadwyn. Basheba stopped the car but didn't turn off the engine. Not until the morbidly obese woman coaxed them over with a heavily tattooed arm.

"Welcome!" she beamed. "Come in, come in."

"I don't like this," Basheba muttered. "Nothing good ever comes from someone being that happy to see me."

Cadwyn leaned toward her and whispered, "We're paying her to be nice to us."

"Right. Hospitality. Everyone get out of my car."

They all piled out, each one only having a single bag of belongings. Buck was the only one excited to be free of the vehicle. With a delighted yelp, he bounded around the yard, trying to jump on and sniff everything at once.

"My, what a big boy he is," the hostess said as she came down from the patio.

"He's a sweetheart," Basheba said. "I'll clean up after him. Oh, you're talking about Cad."

She turned to find the woman beaming up at a very nervous looking Cadwyn. Forcing a polite smile, he glanced to Basheba for help. *He'll face down a demon without blinking,* Basheba thought as she hurried over to close ranks. *But someone shows him some physical interest and he's terrified.* She would have walked over to save him, but the hostess quickly became distracted with Mina, so she took her time wandering closer.

"Aren't you just the prettiest thing?" she said, snatching up Mina's hands and drawing them out wide to get a better look. "How exotic. I bet all the boys swoon over you. Hawaiian?"

"Filipino," Mina replied.

The way Mina managed to keep both her polite smile and tone left Basheba rather impressed. The woman spent a moment gushing on about Ozzie before noticing Basheba. Leaning forward and bracing her hands on her knees wasn't enough to bring them to the same height.

"Hello, sweet angel. I'm Whitney. You are?"

"In my twenties," Basheba replied with a sugary sweetness. "Did you not see me driving the car?"

Whitney's expression soured. "Right."

"I apologize," Cadwyn cut in smoothly. "It's been a long drive."

"I understand." Though she had smiled warmly to Cadwyn as she answered him, her expression cooled when she looked back down to Basheba. "It would be a sore spot for me too."

Cadwyn gripped Basheba's shoulder. If Whitney noticed, she didn't say anything.

"All right. So, why don't we get you all checked in, I'll give you a tour, and then we can have some tea?"

Basheba smiled. "Oh, I know the perfect blend."

CHAPTER 5

Bunches of dried lavender hung about the room, filling the air with their scent and stealing what little headroom Cadwyn had. The whole building, while quaint and beautiful, was designed for people closer to Basheba's height.

Ozzie giggled from the other twin bed. "You're not going to fit on that thing."

"I have noticed that, thank you."

The door opened and the girls rushed in.

"Whitney is already riding my last nerve," Basheba said.

"What a surprise," Mina replied.

Basheba turned around to eye the woman as Buck launched himself onto Cadwyn's bed, kicking and squirming until every item on the mattress had been knocked to the floor. But it was impossible to be mad when the dog confronted Cadwyn with those big brown eyes.

"Who was the last person you got along with at first sight?" Mina asked.

The response was instant, "Buck."

The dog yelped and bounded over to his owner, where he promptly sat and waited to be lavished with attention. She didn't make him wait long.

"Did you guys get the bigger room?" Ozzie asked.

Before they could respond, Whitney called them back down the stairs and the tour began. The layout was simple, with the dining room taking up most of the lower floor. First, Whitney took them to the extension attached to the back of the house. A long dining table, already set with fine china and decorated with fresh flowers, filled up most of the space. The far wall was exposed brick, broken up by a large hearth. A few overstuffed chairs and a low bookshelf made it a sitting area. Cadwyn was grateful to enter the sunroom, hoping to escape the overwhelming scent of lavender, and was struck with the aroma of daisies. He rushed forward to hold the door open for everyone, desperate for some fresh air. The others took it as an act of a gentleman and he wasn't inclined to tell them otherwise. As before, Buck sprinted out. His paws dug into the earth as he brought himself to an abrupt stop.

"Buck," Basheba called to him instantly.

Instead of turning to her, his attention remained locked on the distance. Following his line of sight, Cadwyn noticed rows of small white boxes. The wind changed and brought with it the scent of honey and the steady drone of bees.

"Are those beehives?" Mina asked, her face paling.

If she hadn't already had a deep phobia of bees, her time in the woods would have been enough to change that. The Witch had forced her to confront a hanging man half gouged out by a swarm. Cadwyn had been on the ground during the incident and still had memories of it. Wordlessly, he slipped closer to Mina's side. Not crowding her, but making sure he was in arms reach should she need it.

"Yes. We like to keep things as natural as possible, so we cultivate several hives to pollinate our orchard," Whitney said, sweeping an arm out toward the white boxes as if she was a game show host. "You'll be able to taste their honey with your afternoon tea. Oh, beautiful, are you feeling all right?"

"I'm allergic," Mina said smoothly.

Smart girl, Cadwyn thought to himself. The Witch already knew their deepest fears but no good could come from broadcasting them to the locals.

"Don't you worry, darling," Whitney assured. "They're very polite. They'll keep to their business if you keep to yours."

"As most insects do," Basheba mumbled.

Whitney's hospitable smile slipped as she glared at Basheba. She soon remembered, though, and fixed it back into place.

"Let me give you a tour of the gardens."

"Thanks," Ozzie rushed to say, glancing over at Basheba to see if she would go along with it.

She's going to want to know the layout, Cadwyn thought just as Basheba slipped into her sweet little girl persona. The one she pulled out when she wanted to butter people up. The one that had the local police thinking she was a child.

"Oh, all the trees look so pretty. Can we go down this way?" she asked, pointing off in a seemingly general direction.

They shuffled off and Cadwyn threw Mina an encouraging smile. She barely noticed him as her eyes remained locked on the beehives.

"I'm okay," Mina assured.

Cadwyn gently touched her arm and said, "That changes, I'm right here."

Suddenly, she snapped her gaze up to meet his. "Thank you."

"Anytime." He gave her forearm a gentle squeeze. "Come on, let's get the hell away from those things. They give me the creeps."

In an attempt to make her laugh, he presented her with his arm. She rolled her eyes at him, but he figured that was close enough. He'd take what he could get. Looping her arm around his, they hurried to catch up with the others. After a few feet, he realized one of their party had yet to move. Buck remained rooted to the spot, his head still high and alert, his ears twitching with every slight sound.

"Buck, come on, boy." When he didn't respond, he attempted one of the whistle's he'd heard Basheba use in the past.

"What was that command?" Mina asked when Buck ignored them.

"I don't know."

She looked at him like he was an idiot. "You remember that he's trained to maul people, right?"

"Clearly, I forgot that," Cadwyn said before raising his voice. "Buck! Heel!"

For an instant, Buck's obedience training took over and he ran a few paces toward them. When he realized it wasn't his beloved Basheba calling him, he locked his legs, and skidded to a stop. All the while, his gaze was fastened on the bees.

"That can't be good," Mina whispered.

Cadwyn twisted around and discovered they were alone. "We need to catch up with the others. Now."

"We can't just leave Buck. Basheba will kill us if anything happened to him."

Cadwyn couldn't say exactly when or how they had assumed responsibility for the dog, but he wasn't about to argue the point. Basheba would probably murder everyone in the tri-state area if anything happened to Buck.

"Come on, let's go!" Cadwyn said, trying to keep the desperation from his voice.

A low whistle drifted from a distant point. Buck took off toward it in a dead sprint, pushing past them, and leaving them alone in seconds.

"Why do I feel betrayed?" Cadwyn asked, watching the dog disappear into the trees.

Mina tugged hard on his arm, trying to pull him out of his thoughts and make him move. They had just passed the first row of trees when they heard it. The low, drowning buzz rushed toward them, filled the trees, lingered in the air. A swarm of thousands. Mina clutched his arm, tightening her grip until even his shirt couldn't protect him from her nails.

"We're okay," he whispered, urging her to move. "Just stay close."

They hurried deeper down the path, hoping to catch sight of the others, but there was no relief from the constant buzz. It was always waiting for them. Surrounding them. Growing stronger until it drowned out every other sound. Movement drifted across the corner of Cadwyn's eyes. He gripped Mina's shoulders tight and brought them both to an abrupt halt.

Panting hard, she moved to throw him a questioning gaze. Even without looking at her, he could tell the instant she saw it. The trees shook as something moved behind them. Its milky skin blended in with the surrounding trees, making it impossible to get a proper grasp of its size or shape. But, by the shake of the trees, he knew it was far bigger than either of them. And it was circling them. Gruff snorts and bovine bellows drifted through the ever-present sound of the bees. Not taking his eyes off of it, Cadwyn arched his spine and whispered in her ear.

"When I say run, you go, and don't stop until you find Basheba."

Mina nodded. He allowed them just long enough to draw in a steadying breath. Then he made the call. They both broke into a sprint, pushing themselves until their lungs burned and their legs struggled to keep up the pace. Cadwyn kept a step behind the teenager and glanced behind.

Thick trees slashed and swayed as the creature barreled past them in pursuit. It closed in fast, consuming the distance between them until the shredded remains of the branches rained down upon them like shrapnel.

Cadwyn pushed Mina's back, forcing her to go faster even though he knew they weren't going to outpace it. With a startled scream, she dropped to the earth. He looked down at her, horrified that he might have tripped her up, and didn't notice the fence she had avoided until he slammed into it. Unrelenting wood slats collided with his hips, while his momentum flipped him forward over the fence. The grass softened the blow, but he still landed hard enough to knock the air from his lungs. Pain exploded along his spine as he rolled up.

The thick wood planks of a white running fence separated them now. Mina was on all fours, her eyes wide as the orchard ripped itself apart behind her.

"Go," he ordered.

It seemed she had been waiting for his permission. Pushing up like a sprinter, she followed the fence line, glancing back once to make sure he was following. The orchard exploded, the trees shedding their blossoms to create a wall of white between them that completely severed her from view.

"Go!"

Shielding his eyes, he fled away from the onslaught, further from the fence and Mina, praying that she had listened to him. Then it all stopped. The shaking trees, the noise, the hailstorm of plant life. The mangled leaves and flowers drifted down to blanket the earth around him, allowing him to see for the first time where he had wandered to. The orchard stood to his left. An empty field stretched out to his right. Then, looming like a beast on the horizon, were the woods that surrounded the town. The ones that butted up against the Witch Woods. Just the sight of it made a chill course down his spine.

Mina was somewhere out of sight. He hoped she had found Basheba. Jogging a few feet along the fence, he eyed the orchard. The space between the rows was completely empty. It gave him enough courage to try jumping back over.

A thunderous snort pushed against his back. He turned in time to see the horns slicing down toward him. Flinging himself to the side, he narrowly missed getting gorged.

The pristine, white bull surged on a few more feet before it managed to bring its tremendous bulk to a stop. Its hooves gouged at the earth. Steam billowed from its snout as it turned its massive head, locking its eyes upon him. Cadwyn bolted for the fence. The bull whirled around with the agility an animal of its size shouldn't be able to possess. With a colossal bellow, it charged after him, easily cutting him off from his escape route. He scrambled back as the beast threw its head about, barely managing to get his foot out of the path of the horns. The tips drove deep into the soil. Hard enough that, for the briefest moment, the bull was locked in place.

Cadwyn took advantage of the moment to throw himself up and start running again. Clumps of damp earth splattered his back as the bull ripped itself free. He forced himself to go faster, knowing there was no real escape. Hot, humid air pushed against his neck. He hurled himself to the side, hitting the ground hard. White-hot pain cut across his thigh, whiting out his vision and making his leg tremble. Blood soaked his jeans, spilling from between his fingers even as he grasped the wound.

Choking on his screams, he looked up to see the bull slowly circling him. Its dark eyes locked onto him as it lowered its head, swiping it back and forth as it paced, hooves clawing at the earth; taking its time as it lined up to charge again. Adrenaline flooded his veins until he was vibrating with it. Cadwyn leaped up, barely feeling the wound as he sprinted across the field. The bull lunged and pulled back.

He realized too late that the animal wasn't trying to kill him. It was herding him. Pushing him closer and closer to the forest wall. He tried to move around it, to slip back to the relative safety of the orchard. The bull cut off his every attempt. He lost ground. All too soon, he had been forced into the long shadows of the towering trees.

The bull's attacks had slowed. It no longer needed to force him to run. Now, it simply paced closer, steadily forcing him to back up, driving him deeper into the shadows. He pried his eyes off of the bull long enough to glance over his shoulder, checking to see how far he had gone. Something stood amongst the trees, its skin darker than the shadows that shrouded it. Twin horns curled out of its forehead to brush against the foliage. While he couldn't see its eyes, he knew it was watching him. He knew beyond a doubt that this was what the bull was driving him toward.

The knowledge froze him in place. Snorting hard, the bull surged forward. An ebony blur streaked across his vision. It launched itself at the bull, latching onto his leg and giving a violent shake. *Buck.* Blood spurted free as the Rottweiler thrashed, widening the wound it had inflicted. The bull bellowed in both fury and agony, slashing at Buck in an attempt to stab him. Buck pulled back but didn't retreat. Blood-stained saliva dripped from his fangs, and he snapped and snarled at the bull.

"Cadwyn!" Basheba's scream dragged his eyes from the standoff before him.

He looked over to find Basheba sprinting across the field, her hair glistening golden in the light, and her lips curled in a savage snarl. In that moment, be it because of desperation or blood loss, he had the strongest urge to cheer her arrival.

"Move, you idiot!" she bellowed.

Snapped from his shock, he raced to catch up with her. Chaos grew behind him, but he refused to look back. His eyes were set on the far gate, the orchard beyond, and he needed to get there before the bull escaped Buck's attack. There was a sharp, pained yelp from somewhere behind him. In an instant, rage replaced the determination on Basheba's face. She reached behind her as she picked up her pace, slipping her hand under her jacket. With a sharp jerk, she pulled free her hunting knife. *How long has she been carrying that?* The thought barely had time to race across his mind before they clashed.

Basheba threw herself at the beast that was running him down. Cadwyn caught her mid-air and attempted to keep going. Simply keeping hold of her proved to be almost impossible. She thrashed and snarled, as ferocious as her dog, and knocked him off balance. They fell and she slipped free of his grasp. Before the bull could strike, Buck attacked from the opposite side, coaxing the bull to swing its head around. Basheba took advantage of the opening, lunging forward to slash her blade across its muscular neck.

It reared back, bucking and kicking its hooves wildly. Cadwyn tackled her out of the way before it could stomp her head. Buck went for its exposed underbelly, forcing it back again. Clasping her hand tightly, Cadwyn ran for the gate again. It took a few hard pulls to make her follow. And, even when she did, her eyes never left Buck.

"It's a trap," he spat out between panted breaths. "We need to fall back."

Basheba licked her lips, desperately trying to force out a whistle and signal her dog, but she was breathing too hard to make it work.

"He'll follow!" Cadwyn snapped.

They raced back, Basheba clutching his hand. Each rumbling growl made her look over her shoulder. He had to continually pull her forward to prevent her from going back.

"He'll follow," he repeated.

When they finally got to the fence, Ozzie and Mina reached out to help them over. Whitney had been slower to come but struggled a bit faster once she realized her bull was injured. Cadwyn looped an arm around Basheba's waist and unceremoniously dumped her over the fence. By the time he was working his long legs over, she had already scrambled back onto her feet and was in the process of climbing back into the paddock. He shoved her hard on her shoulder to keep her out.

"It hurt him!" Basheba roared, her one good eye glaring at the bull with bloodlust. "I'm going to turn it into hamburger!"

With his feet once more securely on the ground, Cadwyn had to pick her up again to drag her away.

"You attacked my bull?" Whitney stammered.

"It attacked me," Cadwyn tried to placate.

The woman wasn't having it. "You shouldn't have been in his field. Call your dog back before he does more damage."

A bellowing bark proved the order to be useless. Buck was already on his way back, muscles rippling under his fur as he ran at a staggering speed. He outpaced the injured bull and hurdled over the gate with ease. Cadwyn glanced back across the field. All the fury had left the bull. It now limped lazily across the grass, licking at its injured leg, and looking utterly confused. Cadwyn searched the tree line beyond it, trying to find a trace of the inky black shadow he had seen before. The adrenaline that had kept him upright faded away and he dropped with a broken cry.

"Are you okay?" Basheba asked breathlessly. "You're bleeding."

"I'm okay," Cadwyn assured as he gripped his wounded thigh. Then it hit him. "You're talking to Buck."

The size difference between Buck and Basheba made it completely unnecessary for her to kneel down to hug his neck. She did so anyway, lovingly patting him and tending to the small, barely visible scrape on his side. The Rottweiler winced.

"I'm sorry, I'm sorry," Basheba said swiftly. "Cadwyn, he's injured. Can you have a look at him?"

"Seriously?"

When she looked at him, he lifted one bloodied hand to prove his point. Mina knelt down beside him, having already ripped the sleeves of her shirt off. She checked the wound.

"Is it deep?" she asked.

"I'll need stitches," he said, gasping sharply as she tied the tourniquet tightly around his thigh.

"Basheba," Ozzie said. "Give me the keys, I'm going to get the car."

Basheba tossed them over to the teen as she moved closer to check on Cadwyn.

"How's my hero?" Cadwyn smiled.

"I'm fine." She paused and smirked. "Oh, you're talking about Buck."

"You should get a tetanus shot," Mina cut in. "I wouldn't trust what's on that bull's horns."

"Oh, he's very clean," Whitney said. "You will be paying for his vet bills, of course."

"Sure thing," Basheba said, her voice tight. "Quick question: where did you get that thing that almost killed my friend?"

Cadwyn could almost see Whitney's mind churning, trying to figure out if she was in any legal trouble. Still, she answered.

"He's a gift from the woods."

Mina whipped around to face her. "What do you mean by that?"

Whitney laughed lightly. "It's just a local saying. You'd be surprised what wanders out of those woods."

Cadwyn glanced back to the shadows on the far side of the field. The creature was gone, but he could still feel it watching him. A cold, gut-twisting glare that left him breathless.

"Yeah. You'd be surprised by what stays inside it."

CHAPTER 6

The last time she had been in Black River, Mina hadn't had the opportunity to meet the local town doctor, but she understood from Cadwyn that he wasn't very good at his job. Even when he had been sitting in a jail cell, nursing the wounds from both crashing his bike and from a minotaur attack, he had still preferred to stitch himself up without anesthetic, rather than deal with the man.

Prepared for him to argue once more against getting medical treatment, Mina pushed the issue, even as Cadwyn insisted he had everything he needed in his medical kit to stitch himself up. Basheba hadn't been of much help, taking Cadwyn at his word that he had the situation under control. Ozzie, however, had aided Mina in reaching the level of nagging necessary to get the man into the car. In the end, it was probably Whitney's presence that made up his mind.

The woman had trailed them to the gravel road where Ozzie had the car waiting, screaming the whole while about the wellbeing of her animal and the necessary vet bills.

Basheba might have hit the woman if Ozzie hadn't positioned himself rather unsubtly between them. In a desperate attempt to get the hostess to back off, Mina mentioned that Cadwyn had the grounds for a negligence lawsuit.

"Your website said we would have full reign of the property, and you failed to mention both the killer swarm, and a clearly dangerous animal behind a flimsy fence," she had argued.

Whitney's cheeks almost went as red as her lipstick.

"He went into the bull's paddock."

"Unlabeled paddock," Mina had snapped, "holding a white bull that easily camouflages with the apple blossoms. After you left us unattended, and unaware."

Mina had thought the woman would back off. Instead, she had thrown herself at Cadwyn, desperate to appease the injured man. After two minutes of that, Cadwyn had crawled into the back of the car himself.

He had spent the drive cleaning and packing the wound with the items from his medical kit. The only thing that stopped him from stitching it up on his own was Mina pointing out that he needed a tetanus shot. And the doctor would insist on looking at the wound before giving it to him. It hadn't taken long for them to reach the doctor's office. In keeping with the town's aesthetic, it had been converted from a two-story historical home. Painted midnight black, it almost seemed superimposed upon the vibrant colors of the treelined street.

In a last attempt to get out of it, Basheba had argued that the second he put his name down, word of their arrival would spread through the town like wildfire. Cadwyn had latched onto the idea. But, at last, the threat of infection from a bull that clearly dug its horns in filth, was enough to silence their protests. At least for a while.

The waiting room was mostly empty. Their only competition for the doctor's time was an elderly woman who looked to be in her nineties, a child with the sniffles, and a farmer who had fallen from a ladder. They moved swiftly into one of the waiting rooms in the back, only to have things lag from there.

After five minutes of waiting in the cramped office, Cadwyn began to fuss. His tourniquet had slowed the bleeding and, with nothing left to do, he began to feel the pain. It also couldn't have been comfortable to be sitting in his underwear, a paper-thin sheet the only thing protecting his modesty, while surrounded by fully dressed people. Every small squirm crinkled the plastic sheeting covering the low table.

"I could have been done by now," Cadwyn muttered.

He tried in vain to find a reclined position that wouldn't leave his legs dangling over the edge. Basheba had claimed what little area was left. She perched on the very end, her knees pulled up to her chest, and her back pressed up against the wall.

"And it would be cheaper," she mentioned. "Unless you have a good health plan."

"I have great coverage," Cadwyn said.

The blonde arched an eyebrow. "Really?"

"I work for the government, Basheba."

She absently ran the tip of one finger around the rim of her eyepatch. "I should get health care. It's just so expensive. I've only got the income from my Instagram sponsors."

Both Mina and Ozzie leaned forward, follow-up questions on their tongues, only to have Cadwyn cut in first.

"We'll get married," he said. "I'll claim you as a dependent."

Struggling to keep a straight face, Basheba jabbed a finger toward the door. "Should we head to the chapel now?"

"Nothing's going on here. Just let me stitch this up and I'll be all set."

Mina sighed loudly. "That has to be the most elaborate way I've ever heard of to get out of something. You'd get married just to do your own stitches?"

"They weren't really going to do it," Ozzie said, for some reason whispering even though there was no hope for privacy.

"Basheba would go through with anything just to prove a point," Mina countered.

"I actually would," she shrugged. Patting Cadwyn on one of his feet, she added, "Not that you wouldn't make a great hubby."

"I'd be perfect for you," Cadwyn said. "Most of the time I'd be in a completely different state. And, once a year, on our anniversary, I'll give you food."

Basheba placed a hand against her heart and made a sweet 'aw' noise that sounded far too strange coming from her mouth.

"We're waiting for the professional," Mina said firmly.

"I'm a professional, too," Cadwyn noted.

Mina leaned against the wall, her arms crossed over her chest, eyeing Buck where he lay curled at Basheba's feet.

"I will admit to having some apprehension over whether or not dogs are allowed in the office."

"Hey, he's cleaner than you are," Basheba snapped. "And if anyone asks, he's an emotional support animal."

"I do feel like he's rooting for me to pull through," Cadwyn smiled. "My new fur step-son."

Ozzie sat on the chair by the door, playing with a rainbow slinky he had found in the toybox. He looked up, frowning slightly.

"What did Basheba mean by 'cheaper?'"

Mina shared some confused glances with the others, not quite sure she had understood the question.

"Ozzie, you know you have to pay to see a doctor, right?" she asked gently.

His face scrunched up. "You do?"

"You came to the hospital with us for your arm," Cadwyn reminded.

"Yeah, that was a weird experience. Normally, Doctor Jenny comes by my house for stuff like that."

Basheba's jaw dropped slightly. Mina had never seen the blonde look so utterly confused. "You've been paying for my medical bills. What did you think that was for?"

"Your eyepatch."

"The bill's over $3,000! You didn't think that was excessive?"

Ozzie shrugged. "How much do eyepatches cost?"

"I got this one for $15."

Ozzie nodded once and pointed to her. "Huh. Yeah, that does seem a bit over the top now that you mention it."

The door opened, severing the conversation and drawing everyone's attention to the nurse who had just entered the room. Mina noticed it was the same woman who had been at the reception desk and wondered how many people were actually working at this practice.

"I'm sorry, the doctor's a little backed up. He sent me in to check on you."

The moment the nurse closed the door, Buck was on his feet. While he didn't growl, it was clear he was agitated, and the change instantly made Mina tense up.

Basheba seamlessly slipped into her darling pre-teen persona, the one that had convinced the woman to let the dog into the room in the first place.

"Buck," Basheba cooed.

The dog dumped its rump onto the floor but kept his deadlock stare. The nurse eyed him with cautious suspicion as she inched around him to reach Cadwyn's side. She eyed the blood-soaked remains of his jeans, which had been left in a tangled lump in the nearby sink. The moment the nurse placed her clipboard down to examine his thigh, Cadwyn snatched it up and quickly read through it.

"The wound looks clean," she said.

"Yeah. I got bored." Cadwyn looked up from the paperwork with a charming smile. "I can do the rest myself if the doctor's busy. All I need is a tetanus shot, and I'll be out of your hair."

"Oh, you're a doctor now?" she teased.

"Nurse," he corrected. "Specializing in psychiatric and emergency care."

The nurse shifted her weight onto one foot and tucked some strands of brunette hair behind her ear.

"That's impressive, Mr." She paused to take the sheet from him and recheck his name. "Winthrop? As in the Bell Witch Winthrops?"

Cadwyn squirmed, struggling to keep hold of his polite smile.

"I guess you could put it that way."

"You're kind of a celebrity around these parts," the nurse said. She placed a hand on his leg casually, keeping the clipboard to her chest. "Did you know that?"

"I've heard rumors."

The nurse inched closer and Cadwyn tensed, his eyes darting to Basheba. The blonde didn't notice his soundless plea for help. But she was paying attention. Patting the back of Buck's head with one hand, her eyes remained locked on the nurse. Mina searched the blonde's face carefully but couldn't catch on to what she was thinking.

"Would I be able to get the supplies, please?" Cadwyn asked, his voice carefully smooth.

"I suppose I can make an exception," the nurse said with a sly smile. "Just this once."

"And the shot?" Basheba asked.

The nurse jumped as if she had forgotten there was anyone else in the room.

"I'll just go grab that, shall I?"

"Please," Cadwyn said, his eyes crinkling around the edges.

The second the door closed after the nurse, he dropped the expression and bolted upright. He instantly caught Basheba's gaze.

"You saw that, right?" he demanded.

"Yep," Basheba chirped, her attention now fixed on the door.

"She was flirting."

"I noticed."

"That's three times now," Cadwyn said. "Three times in two days that strangers have made a pass at me."

"Why does that worry you?" Ozzie asked. "I mean, you're a pretty good-looking guy. In an unconventional way."

Cadwyn's arched an eyebrow and Ozzie waved a hand about his face.

"I think it's your mouth. It's a little too wide. Something's off about your teeth, too."

"They're fake," Cadwyn said, not sure if he should be offended or not.

"My point is that people will want to hit on you. Back me up, Mina."

She glanced at Ozzie, surprised at being brought into the conversation. "I don't see why you two are so tense. It's unprofessional but —"

"Cut and run?" Basheba cut in. The question was clearly directed at Cadwyn alone.

"Pass me my sweatpants."

"What is going on?" Mina asked. "You need medical care. We all agreed on that."

"Oh, my God, you are supposed to be smart." Basheba sighed, pinching the bridge of her nose and squeezing her eyes shut tight. Jumping down from her perch, she flung her arms out. "In this town, when something feels wrong, you don't stick around to see how the situation will shake out. You set something on fire, and you run."

"We're not burning down the doctor's office," Cadwyn said calmly.

She glared at him, her annoyance somewhat lessened as she watched him awkwardly struggle his way into his pants without aggravating his wound.

"Well, if you want to be lazy about the situation," she grumbled.

"Everyone, just stop," Mina snapped. "This is insane. Flirtation doesn't equal a death threat."

"And besides," Ozzie added. "We weren't anywhere near Black River when my friend hit on you. The Witch's influence can't reach that far." His dark eyebrows drew together. "Can it?"

Basheba huffed and proceeded to ignore them both, leaving them with only Cadwyn to turn to for answers. His focus was on getting the drawstring of his pants tied up. Frustration bubbled inside of Mina. *If the Witch could manipulate people from such distances, surely she would have before.* Years of research washed through her skull, dredging up a term from the depths of her mind — *Folie à deux; madness shared by two.* It was clear that the more time they spent together, the more they fed into each other's paranoia. For a moment, another term threatened to distract her. *Folie à famille; the psychological theory that a family can share a madness.* It had been one of her first exploitations for her family's belief in The Bell Witch. That each generation had taught their children to fear the monster in the dark. *Things had been simpler then.* Still, she wasn't ready to give up on common sense altogether.

"Can we at least try to use logic here?" she asked.

Basheba huffed louder. "Fine, Mina. What do you suggest?"

"We at least steal the meds we need before we leave. You know, so he doesn't die of infection in the Witch Woods?"

The blonde blinked at her then grinned broadly. "Am I starting to like you?"

"That's a terrifying thought."

"I can leave some money, you know, so they won't call the cops," Ozzie offered.

"Yeah, okay, I suppose," Basheba said. "Sucks all the fun out of the situation, though."

Not wanting to deal with that conversation, Mina headed for the door. "I'll go grab the shot."

"Do you know what you're looking for?" Cadwyn asked.

"My cousin got it a few weeks back. I remember what it looks like." For once, her habit of latching onto every possibility to increase her knowledge of medicine was going to come in handy.

"You can't go by yourself," Cadwyn said.

"I'll be fine," Mina assured.

"He means you're going to need someone to distract the nurse," Basheba said. She rolled her good eye. "She's getting the shot, or is supposed to be, so there's a high possibility you're going to cross paths. Have you never stolen anything before?"

"I'll go with her," Ozzie said, hopping up and leaving the slinky on the chair.

"We'll meet you out front," Basheba said.

"Be careful," Cadwyn added.

Basheba smiled. "If you mess this up, just yell for Buck. He'll hear you."

Mina was surprised by how comforting she found that notion. Trying not to show it, she cracked open the door and slipped out into the hallway, Ozzie close behind her. The layout of the converted house made sneaking around a lot easier. Since the living room served as both the reception area and waiting room, they had a wall and some distance away from any prying eyes. Mina jerked her head down the hall and Ozzie took off first, as silent as a ghost. Leaving the door slightly ajar, Mina followed.

Doors lined the hallway. Ozzie paused at each one to press his ear against it, checking for any traces of noise before opening the door enough to glance inside. Mina copied the process on the other side of the hallway. She wasn't sure what the nurse had meant by having a backlog, because it seemed like every room they checked was an empty doctor's room.

At the very end, the hallway diverged into a T-intersection, leaving one room on each side, both without doors. Ozzie took the right and Mina the left. Moving unintentionally in unison, they both pressed themselves against their assigned wall and carefully craned their necks to peek around the corner. She was disappointed to find a dimly lit laundry room. Just a slab of cement, a few machines, and a back door with rusted hinges. Slightly discouraged, she turned to tell Ozzie and found him darting across the narrow corridor, his eyes wide and his arms flying about with barely contained frantic energy.

She didn't have time to ask the question before he barreled her into the laundry room. They scrambled to cram themselves behind the small strip of wall beside the door. There was hardly enough room to hide them both. They froze as footsteps shuffled out of the opposite room and disappeared down the hallway. Ozzie slumped and whispered.

"Exactly how illegal is this?"

"So far, we're just trespassing," she replied. "But I'm sure our lawyer can argue that we just got turned around."

Ozzie's eyes remained wide as he nervously chewed on his bottom lip. Several moments later, he curled slightly to look out into the hallway, checking to see if it was empty. He nudged her with his elbow, and she moved so she could see what he saw. The same nurse from before disappeared into the waiting room. An instant later, she rushed back out, heading to the reception desk. They barreled across the hallway and into the medical supply closet. Without a word of discussion, Ozzie took a sentry position by the threshold, allowing Mina to search the array of glass door cabinets. She ran her finger along the glass, tracing the bottle's labels, slightly horrified to feel the door rattle under her fingertip.

"She didn't even lock it? That's insane."

"Mina," Ozzie hissed. "Just take the win."

"Right. Sorry. Hold on, they don't even have a door for their drug room? That's got to be some kind of medical malpractice."

"Mina," Ozzie said through clenched teeth, his eyes almost bulging out of his head.

"Sorry, sorry," she stammered and forced herself to refocus.

Perusing the cabinet and the array of medications, it struck her that the vast majority of the vials were slender single-use tubes. *Doesn't anyone get sick in this town?*

"Mina," Ozzie's voice barely carried over the hum of the distant air conditioner.

She sped up her search, scanning the neat rows, searching for a green edged label that matched her memory.

"Mina," Ozzie repeated, his voice becoming ever softer.

"Hold on," she whispered back. She could barely contain her squeal of joy when she pushed up onto her toes and spotted the matching colored label. "Found it."

Thrusting open the glass door, she reached deep into the back of the cabinet and plucked out a half dozen vials.

"Mina."

Flushed with victory, she turned to answer him and saw the pure fear on the boy's face. His gaze was locked on a spot beyond her left shoulder.

A cold gush of air washed across the back of her neck. She froze, tightening her grip around the vials until her fingers ached. All of her focus narrowed down upon the singular task of controlling her breathing. As if she could master everything around her if she could only slow her breathing.

Her attempts to think were derailed the moment the thumping began, erratic, dull, and heavy. Something was slamming hard against the wood sides of the cabinets behind her. The vials rattled against each other with a metallic click.

Curiosity ate at her insides. The muscles in her neck strained with the urge to turn and see what was behind her. Ozzie yelped with surprise as she suddenly bolted for the door. Unable to get out of the way, she crashed into him and they both tumbled onto the hallway floor in a tangled mess of limbs. Still clutching the vials, she rolled off of the stunned boy. Somehow, Ozzie was the first one to his feet, already tugging at her arm as the thudding sound grew louder.

Getting her feet back under herself, she couldn't resist the temptation to look back. The cabinet that had been behind her was scraping across the floor, pushed from behind by a clustered array of pale limbs. Thin and pale under soggy clumps of dirt, the arms clawed and thudded against the cabinet walls. Their nails cracked in their desperation. It was as if several children were trapped behind the thick piece of furniture. The cabinet legs scraped against the tiled floor, releasing a wild squeal that cut through the increasing thuds. The vials rattled violently as the cabinet loomed over her.

"Mina!" Ozzie cried, snapping her out of her shock.

His hard tug forced her to her feet and she staggered to keep from falling onto her face. She dug in her heels and threw her weight back, forcing him to trip backward.

"Back door," she said.

They sprinted away just as the cabinet reached the threshold of the closet. Filthy limbs lashed out, scraping at the thin carpet and trying to trip them. A voice called them back. Mina didn't look to see if it was the children or the staff. They darted through the laundry room and slammed through the back door. Once more, no one had thought to lock it. Hands battered the frosted windows that speckled the back of the house. Their touch left smears of dirt and blood.

Still clutching each other's hands, both Mina and Ozzie staggered to a stop. She wanted to go right, him left, and they were left stranded just beyond the door. It was as if being drenched in warm sunlight tricked their brains into thinking they were safe. The door suddenly wrenched open. Limbs filled the space. Squirming, writhing, clutching at the frame until the plaster and wood cracked within their grip.

Children. They're all children. The thought speared Mina's mind, a spike of fear hurling her from her shock. Ozzie felt the same impulse and they shoved at each other, each deciding to go the way the other had suggested. Legs and faces began to squeeze through the mass. Ozzie released Mina's hands and began to push at her back, shoving her hard to the left. The limbs followed them as they fled around the corner of the building. Every window was filled with limbs. Drowned, gargling shrieks filled the air around them. Ozzie's hands became a constant weight against her spine. The contact seemed like her only tie to reality. The only thing she knew was real.

Basheba already had the car idling at the curb, with the hatch trunk and the front passenger door open wide. Ozzie jumped into the front passenger seat while Mina scrambled into the back, careful to avoid clashing with Buck or Cadwyn as she did so. The moment both doors were closed, Basheba pulled out into the street, barely checking for traffic.

"What happened?" Cadwyn asked, one hand protectively clasping his wound.

Mina presented him with the vials she had protected so carefully. It hurt to relax her fingers.

"I'm pretty sure Katrina knows we're in town," Ozzie said between heavy, panted breaths.

"I told you so," Basheba replied in a sing-song tone.

Even Cadwyn was stunned into silence by the reaction, leaving enough silence for her to add almost cheerfully.

"I'm hungry. Who wants breakfast?"

CHAPTER 7

Cadwyn had learned long ago to never go anywhere without an impressively stocked first aid kit. It didn't matter where he was going, he always had his bag close at hand. Most people he knew in his day to day life assumed he was either a hypochondriac or a doomsday survivalist. Anyone with knowledge of The Witch thought he was responsible. In truth, it was his safety blanket. But that didn't keep him from taking a great deal of pride in his kit. Adding the numerous, stolen vials of Tetanus vaccine to the kit made him brim with pride. He felt like a collector with a new prized piece.

Basheba pulled up into the town's supermarket parking lot and killed the engine while he was still fussing over his new addition. She twisted around in her seat and chirped with a smile.

"Need any help?"

"You just want to stab me repeatedly," he replied.

"Damn, foiled again."

He chuckled at that, awkwardly stretching out on the mattress Basheba used as a bed to slip his sweatpants down. His long legs got tangled up in Basheba's sleeping bag. That, combined with the position of the wound, made the whole process painfully difficult.

"Can I help?" Mina asked, barely able to contain her excitement.

He frowned at her.

"The stitching, I mean. Not the pants," she clarified. "For medical practice."

With one last yank, he managed to free himself from his sweatpants. "Have you even sutured an orange before?"

"No," she admitted sheepishly.

Heaving a sigh, he tossed the pants behind him and jerked his chin to the overstuffed medical bag. "Sanitize your hands."

"Seriously?"

"I'll let you do the needle," he clarified.

She was a good nurse. Attentive, sure, and with an iron stomach. Although, he knew that already. Their last encounter during the Harvest had given her more than enough opportunities to prove herself. From the firestorm of poisonous gas of Basheba's making, to the wounds inflicted upon them by The Witch. Her thirst for experience and knowledge was something he could indulge. It was a tether that he felt could solidify into a real bond, if nurtured correctly.

Only a few days before, he had managed to get his hands on a local anesthetic, a gift from a doctor friend who could legally buy it. It kept him from having to steal some from work. He allowed Mina to prepare the syringe, watching carefully as she followed each of his instructions to the letter. Completely focused, she slowly inserted the needle into his flesh. He flinched. She froze.

"Sorry, did that hurt?"

"You're stabbing his open wound," Ozzie said, his suddenly pale skin looking clammy under a fine sheen of emerging sweat. "I don't think it's going to tickle."

"You're doing fine," Cadwyn assured her while effortlessly threading a needle with his gloved hands. "Just keep your hand steady as you take it out."

Mina nodded. Returning her laser focus to the task at hand, she kept her hand as still as stone as she pushed the plunger. Slow and steady, she pulled the needle out. The pace allowing him to feel the movement. It didn't waver at all.

"You're going to be a good surgeon," he said.

"You think so?" She grinned happily. "Thanks for letting me do this."

He dismissed that with a wave of his hand. "How else are you supposed to learn?"

"Most people would say in a classroom?" Mina chuckled.

Cadwyn paused, once more realizing how far some of his life experiences were from others. It was so easy to forget when surrounded only by the families.

"I suppose that's one way."

"How did you learn?" she asked, voice still warm and tickling with laughter.

Cadwyn didn't have it in him to ruin it, not if she was smiling after what had just happened. Basheba made a different decision.

"I'm guessing by doing it on himself," she called from the front seat.

Cadwyn shot her a glare. For once, it was enough to make the blonde look somewhat remorseful.

"Sorry," she mouthed.

"On yourself?" Mina asked.

It was possible to see the exact moment she recalled the tales of his childhood. Stories of the last man standing. He didn't blame his family for eventually leaving his brother's side. Each of them had other people they needed to protect. Or they couldn't witness him slowly being torn apart, body and soul, by Katrina's demons. He could understand it. But he could never have done it. No matter what it cost him, he couldn't have left his brother alone. *Not until the end.*

"Oh, I'm sorry. I didn't mean —"

Cadwyn nudged her with his good foot to break off her stammering.

"My brother taught me how to do this. It's a good memory. One I'm happy to revisit. Now," he said as he held up the needle with one hand and smacked his thigh with the other, "drugs have taken effect. So, hand me the tweezers and watch closely. We're doing a simple continuous stitch."

The bull's horn had been sharp enough to leave a straight, clean-edged cut. Coagulation had done its part, slowing the flow of blood from a constant pour to a trickling weep. He allowed Mina to clean the smears left behind by the gauze and pinched one side of the wound. The flesh offered little resistance for the needle and offered a small droplet of blood to slick its passing.

A low, sickly moan made him freeze. He snapped around, unable to see Ozzie in the front seat as he doubled over, desperately trying to stifle his gag reflex. *He's scared of blood.* In all the chaos, Cadwyn had completely forgotten. Guilt trickled, thick and hot, into Cadwyn's stomach at his utter lack of care for the teenager. Before he could think of anything to say, Basheba had already sat up, forcing a very disgruntled Rottweiler to crawl over Ozzie's back. The teen's whimpers cut sharply into gasps for air against the dog's weight.

"Well, I'm officially hungry. And since I'd get dirty looks if I didn't get food for everyone, I'm going to need someone to carry the bags. Ozzie, you up for it?"

The teen lunged on the face-saving excuse to leave and was out of the car before Buck had time to get off of his back. Basheba somewhat gracefully crawled into the driver's seat again.

"If anyone has an allergy or dietary restrictions, say it now or go hungry. I'm not doing two trips."

"Nothing deep-fried, please," Mina said.

"I hate coconut," Cadwyn reminded.

At the wave of her hand, Basheba coaxed Buck from the car. "Deep-fried, coconut. Got it."

Cadwyn smirked, tipping his head to catch sight of Ozzie through one of the windows. Color was already coming back to his cheeks.

"Thanks, Basheba," Cadwyn said.

Half out the door, she gave him a furrowed look. "Yeah, I was trying to provoke a different kind of response."

She slammed the door.

"I know you're a good person," he called out, trying his best to mimic her previous sing-song tone.

Her muffled voice drifted through the partially open window, "You can't prove a thing."

Chuckling to himself, he held out the needle and tweezers to Mina.

68

"I'm in a good mood," he said. "Give it a whirl, Crane."

***

Ozzie rushed to the supermarket's automatic doors, only stopping when they opened and a wave of chilled air smacked him in the face. Basheba wasn't about to jog to catch up, not until Buck decided they were racing. Then she broke into a sprint, pushing herself until her lungs were burning, even though she never had a chance of winning. The dog spent the extra time waiting for her by body slamming Ozzie for attention. One of his leaps made the door open again and he trotted inside.

"Is he allowed to do that?" Ozzie asked.

Basheba shrugged as she crossed the threshold. "Who's going to stop him?"

While the store wasn't crowded by any measure, there were enough people milling about that she was able to track the path Buck had taken. The people he passed all stopped to glare in his general direction, clearly not sure how to react. A short snort escaped her.

"Like a dog in a store is the weirdest thing they've seen in this town," she muttered to Ozzie.

When she didn't get a reply, she lightly patted him on the back.

"Stop beating yourself up. So you don't like seeing someone getting jabbed. So what? Otherwise, you did well today."

"I didn't do much," Ozzie grumbled.

"You got the meds, didn't you?"

"Mina got them," Ozzie said, somewhat distracted as he watched Basheba get a shopping trolley.

It's probably the first time he's ever been grocery shopping.

"And you got Mina out," she countered. "Don't brag about things you didn't do, but don't be afraid to claim the things you did."

Basheba pushed the cart toward him. While he looked at it like it was alien technology, he soon got the hang of it and followed her into the low aisles.

"Why do you think I got Mina out?" he asked.

"Because she's a Freezer," Basheba scoffed.

"A what?"

"A Freezer." She walked sideways to better watch his reactions. "You know, like how everyone has a default 'F?'"

"I've got no idea what you're talking about."

"Survival instincts," she said. A few gasped cries let her know that Buck was still lurking nearby. "Flight and Fight get the most screen time, but there's also Freeze and Friend. Each has its perks and drawbacks depending upon the situation. My uncle, the good one, the dead one, he had this theory that everyone has a default 'F.' And you've got to know yours if you're going to master your reactions."

"How was I supposed to know that?" Ozzie dismissed the question and quickly asked another. "Mina is a Freezer?"

"I think it's because she's an analytical thinker," Basheba said, tossing a few bags of chips into the cart. "She can't react to anything until she's convinced herself she's actually seeing it."

"And you're a Fighter," Ozzie said carefully, as if he wasn't quite sure how Basheba would react.

"Bold and impulsive," Basheba chirped. "It's not a bad thing. None of them are."

Ozzie's gaze lowered to his hands. "It seems better to be a Fighter."

"Yeah, it's great when you're confronted with demons from the depths of hell determined to rip your soul apart. Not so much when it turns out they're just a family trying to celebrate Billy's sixth birthday."

Basheba cringed at the memory.

Ozzie's eyes grew wide. "What did you do to Billy's family?"

"Don't worry about it," she dismissed and picked up her pace. "My point is, I'm pretty sure whatever shook you guys up at the doctor's office had Mina standing like a deer in the headlights. If you weren't there, she probably wouldn't have gotten back to the car. Whatever else happens, you can be proud of that."

The metal wire of the shopping cart was cool against her hands as she gripped it and hopped up onto the front rail. After she had crawled over the edge and stood in the main barrel, she was tall enough to grab the box of cereal she had wanted from the top shelf. She tossed it in with the chips and didn't bother to get out.

"What would you classify Cadwyn as? A Fighter, right?"

Basheba should have expected the question. It was pretty obvious that the teenager had a bit of a man-crush on the older nurse. *I wonder if it'll develop into a bromance or hero-worship?*

"According to my awesome dead uncle," Basheba said, coaxing Cadwyn to turn the corner. "He was born with the *friend* impulse."

"Friend?" He sounded a little disappointed.

"Approach your fear with compassion and restraint," Basheba recited the words her uncle had told her so long ago. Memories consumed her mind until her nose filled with the phantom aroma of s'mores and overcooked hot dogs. She could feel the heat of the campfire against her cheek, hear his voice that always seemed to grumble like a bear. "Then try to understand them and give them what they need."

Ozzie's question snapped her back to reality. "Who actually reacts that way to anything?"

My uncle. "The bravest people I know," she said instead. "To confront your fears without panic. To try and find something good about the thing that terrifies you. I've tried, a lot, and have never once succeeded in pulling it off."

"But he was pretty active in the woods," Ozzie protested, as if still slightly offended on Cadwyn's behalf.

"Your first impulse isn't your only one. You can learn to challenge it and Cadwyn's done just that. Actually, I've never even heard of anyone being able to fight their defaults the way he does." Her spike of pride faltered as she recalled, "But I guess he learned the hard way."

"What do you mean?"

"A Friend's strength is either in finding compassion and mercy, or outlasting their fear until it gets bored and slithers off somewhere. You can't befriend a demon. And they don't get bored. Oh! Down this aisle, I want some granola bars."

Ozzie's footsteps slowed.

"How can you talk about this stuff so easily?" Ozzie asked.

"Fear theory?"

"The demons," he said in a sharp, low whisper.

She shrugged one shoulder. "Oh, that. It's just practice, Ozzie. Live with us long enough and you'll get the hang of it, too."

Buck's yelp drew her attention to the end of the aisle. She tossed some instant noodles into the cart as her large Rottweiler rounded the corner and hurried over, his nails frantically clacking upon the tiles.

"Hey there, beautiful," she grinned, leaning over to pat him.

"Are you its owner?" The sharp voice came from a woman who was clearly trailing after Buck. The woman jabbed a finger accusingly at Buck while also trying to soothe the screaming toddler perched in the shopping cart's seat.

"I'm not a fan of the whole 'master-pet' dynamic," Basheba replied, balling her hand into a fist and holding it by Buck's snout. It didn't take him more than a second to understand that command, and he batted her hand with the back of his paw, almost like a fist-bump. "We're just really good bros."

"But he is yours?" the woman snapped.

For a moment, the woman turned her full attention to her toddler, allowing Basheba an opportunity to squirm a little further away from the approaching screaming lump of fat and drool.

"You can't bring your animal in here," the woman said at last.

"Why not? You brought yours."

Horrified outrage twisted up the woman's face. "Charles is a *baby*."

"Buck is housebroken," Basheba countered. "Seems like that's the better option."

The woman puffed up her chest. "You can't have dogs around food."

Admittedly, Basheba was having a bit too much fun antagonizing the stranger. *Any opportunity to ruin the day of a Black River native.*

"Everything is packaged. It's fine."

"What about the fresh produce? He'll drool all over them."

Heaven forbid something tarnish the local crops, she scoffed internally. "He drools less than your crotch-goblin. Any chance you could get it to shut up some time soon?" For added emphasis, she patted the head of her obedient and silent pup.

"I'm going to call the manager on you."

"Oh, no," Basheba droned lazily.

"And I'm going to call the police."

"Okay."

The lady stomped her foot in frustration and pulled her mobile phone from her purse. "I'm calling them right now. What's your name?"

Basheba leaned forward, resting her arms on the edge of the railing and making sure she had a perfect view of the fallout before she answered the question. As expected, the woman's eyes grew wide when she recognized the last name.

"Bell?"

Basheba nodded happily. "That's me."

Without a word, the woman turned her cart around and rushed off back around the corner, picking the quickest route to get out of Basheba's sight.

"What just happened? I thought we were celebrities," Ozzie said.

"For some," she said. "For others, we're a living Chernobyl site. There's no safe place around us."

Glancing down, she grinned at her dog and patted her thigh. He leaped into the cart without hesitation. If it wasn't for Ozzie's death grip on the handle, it would have toppled over. As it was, Basheba ended up squeezed into a corner, helpless prey for Buck's attention. He licked her face without remorse.

"We should probably get some drinks, and maybe some fruit," Ozzie said.

"Canned fruit is the next aisle over."

"What about real fruit?"

"From this town?" Basheba scoffed. "Why not just take a cyanide tablet? At least that way you'll get to feel like a Soviet spy."

"I ate food here last time."

"At the family barbeque?"

He nodded, eyes a little too wide.

"Yeah, the Sewalls put on a good spread," Basheba noted. "They bring everything in from out of town."

Whatever comfort Ozzie might have got from that faded away when they rounded the corner and entered a more open setting in the supermarket, where the fresh produce butted up against the fridges. It made it impossible to mistake that they were now the center of attention. A cold lump forged in the pit of Basheba's stomach as she surveyed the gathering before her. Some only snuck quick glances. Others stared without restraint.

"Maybe we should just get the drinks and go," Ozzie whispered. "I'm sure Cadwyn and Mina are getting hungry."

"Yeah," Basheba replied. Abruptly, she shook off the creepy feeling and turned around to check. "You're paying, right?"

"I can," he stammered, somewhat confused.

"What?" She put on the Tennessee twang that constant travel had dulled over the years. "I might be cheap, baby boy, but I ain't free."

Ozzie scrunched up his nose and rolled his eyes. But there was also a smile in there and she figured that was a good sign. *At least he's not afraid. Now I just have to make sure he stays that way until we're back out in the open.*

Perched in the shopping cart, she used her extra height to scan the building as best she could. While they had people's attention, no one ventured too close, giving Ozzie a free path down the last aisle. They didn't stop. Basheba just tipped the bottles into the cart as they passed. Buck grumbled in protest and propped his front paws on the railing, nudging Basheba aside to make more room for himself. Barely any time had passed before they were approaching the checkout.

Basheba straightened abruptly when she noticed it. The silence. No talk or chatter to dull the scrape of the shopping cart wheels. Even the ambient music pumped through the old speaker system had died away. The baby had stopped its squalling. Everything was just suddenly still.

Basheba twisted around, checking to see if Ozzie had noticed it, too. As she locked eyes with him, the first note rang out. A metallic twang like an old music box that resonated off the barren walls. The first strike didn't have time to fade away before it was met with another, and another, all clustering together to create a tune she had known since childhood. It was Katrina's music box. The gift she gave to each of her chosen few, marking them for selection, drawing them back to the woods. Her music boxes with demons lurking inside.

Ozzie had only heard the music for one season, and yet it struck him instantly. His hands gripped the handle of the cart so tightly his knuckles threatened to split the skin. Buck began to growl, long and low, the sound barely rising above the twang of the music box's melody.

"Don't suppose you're up for just running with the food," Basheba said.

"We have to pay. I mean, we have time, right? It's just a few things. Better than security snatching us up and making us sit in an office for a while."

She rolled her eyes. *Bloody Sewalls.*

"Fine," she grudgingly accepted. "But we're doing this fast or I'm leaving you behind."

His hard swallow seemed to echo over their silent audience, "That sounds fair."

Without warning, Ozzie sprinted for the counter. The sudden lurch caught both of the cart's passengers off guard. They stumbled back, throwing their combined weight against the side of the shopping cart and knocking it out of Ozzie's control. They sideswiped a display of nail polish remover bottles, sending them scattering across the floor. Making no attempt to gather them up, Ozzie pushed on to the counter, apologizing profusely every step of the way. Buck leaped from the cart as Basheba gathered their shopping up into one armful and dumped them onto the counter. The checkout clerk eyed them suspiciously from under his dark mop of hair.

"Instead of scanning each one, how about we just shove an obscene amount of money at you, and you keep whatever's leftover as a tip?"

He scoffed. "How will I know what's the tip if I don't put them through. You're not that bright, are you?"

Basheba pressed her lips into a tight smile. "Too bad. He's loaded."

Unimpressed, the clerk started to scan the items, deliberately going a little slower than necessary. All the while, the music played. Each 'ping' of the machine interrupted the flow of the song that was now playing in earnest through the old speakers. Basheba restlessly tried to keep track of everyone surrounding them.

It was the anticipation that killed her. Helplessly waiting for Katrina to make her move. Restricted to reaction instead of action. The weight of her hunting knife against her spine was a constant and comforting pressure. Her hand twitched to reach back and touch it. Still, the music played. Basheba took note of the volume, determined to bolt if it got any louder. There were too many aisles, too many places for things to hide. Too many people. But the song still hadn't grown louder by the time they were halfway through checkout. It wasn't comforting. Tension twisted around her gut like barbed wire.

Katrina wouldn't let a chance like this slip past. Basheba scanned the room, her fingers twitching with the desire for action. *So what's the go, Katrina? Are you going to make your move? Are you too weak after the doctor's office?* The thought made her smile, even though she couldn't bring herself to believe it.

Scanning the room again, she noticed the man working his way toward the door. It was impossible not to. He was a giant minotaur of a man. Big and broad, with biceps that threatened to split his shirt sleeves even as they hung loosely at his side. His heavy brow lowered like a cliff ridge over his dark eyes, casting them into shadows as he glared back at her. A cluster of other men started to drift out from the depths of the building, gathering like waterdrops in front of the only exit. The large man nodded to the clerk, and the boy's movements slowed to a crawl.

She caught Ozzie's gaze. He had been too pre-occupied with completing the task before him that he hadn't yet noticed the gathering men.

"We need to go," Basheba told him in a whisper. "Now."

Ozzie nodded once, tossed Basheba his wallet, and started gathering up whatever items had already been processed.

"I haven't finished yet," the clerk said when Basheba thrust a credit card into his face.

"We don't want the rest," she replied.

The worker didn't take the card.

"You wanted me to ring you through," he said. "I'm going to ring you through."

"No. We're checking out. Now."

He stared down at her, clearly expecting some kind of social protocol to kick in and have her back down. *Politeness has killed too many of my relatives for me to care, buddy boy.* When it dawned on him that she wasn't going to give way, his gaze flicked over her shoulder. Basheba slammed her hand down on the countertop, creating a loud thwack that resonated through the building. The clerk jumped along with Ozzie.

"Who is he?" Basheba asked.

"Just a friend."

Basheba bit a smile. "Your friend's blocking the door."

"It's a free country."

"It's a democracy," Basheba corrected. "If it were free, I'd be able to do whatever the hell I wanted without consequences."

She ignored the look Ozzie threw her way.

"Aren't you Bells used to that sort of thing?" the clerk asked.

Basheba tilted her head to the side. The clerk arched an eyebrow in challenge.

"You're a Bell, right? Basheba."

When Basheba didn't reply, the clerk smiled like he had won a small victory.

"Well, Bells are used to getting their way. Historically, I mean."

Basheba's continued silence irked him.

"With Katrina Hamilton," he pressed, fishing for a response.

She couldn't help but bite. "You must have failed so many history classes."

"I know the real history. Not the lies and misinformation your family spread."

"Oh, you're an idiot," she said as if she had just solved a puzzle. "Ring us out. Now."

The clerk bristled at the dismissal and snatched up the card. He didn't process it through, however. "Katrina Hamilton was just an old widow. A healer working with herbs. The Bell's swindled her out of her land, and when she stood up for her rights, you accused her of witchcraft."

"My *ancestors* accused her," Basheba cut in with a bitter smirk. "Supposedly."

"There's not supposedly about it. They're called facts."

Basheba laughed. "Quick note. By your version of events, she died an innocent woman. Then, while dead, learned witchcraft and came back as a ghost. What an overachiever."

The clerk's smug smile curled into a bitter frown. "After what she endured, I'm not surprised."

No matter how many times she encountered it, Basheba was never fully prepared for the complete lack of doubt present in the Black River citizens. There was no discussion about the reality of ghosts. No hesitation to believe. Pushing aside her momentary surprise, Basheba tipped her head to the men at the door again.

"And what about those guys? They part of your little delusional cult as well?"

"What cult?" the clerk asked.

"Basheba." Ozzie's warning made her realize just how many people were around them now. Still at a distance, but undeniably staring. Enough men had now gathered by the door that they blocked the only exit. They whispered amongst themselves, the words lost under the music box's melody.

Basheba felt the pressure building inside of her, as if her blood was suddenly too thick for her veins. The tune played on, an endless loop that worked on her nerves and made her feel the eyes upon her all the more. Carefully, she took in the room, noting the people who had changed their positions. At the remains of the toppled tower of nail polish remover bottles, a small group had gathered, including the woman from before. Her child continued to wail. Red-faced and weeping, it threw its whole body into each gasp and shriek. Basheba couldn't hear any of it. *What else are you changing, Katrina?*

"You got the bags, right, Ozzie?" Basheba asked.

He stammered that he did as she smiled encouragingly.

"Good." Making sure she sounded as pleasant as she could, she reached over and plucked a lighter from the display on the countertop. "This too. Put it through."

The man hesitated and Ozzie snatched the card back, exchanging it for a handful of bills.

"Oh, and this," Basheba added as she bent down and scooped up one of the large plastic bottles of nail polish remover.

She swiped it over the scanner herself then turned on her heel and stalked to the door. Buck was quicker than Ozzie to fall into pace beside her. Already an imposing sight by size alone, Buck lowered his head and bared his teeth. The first traces of doubt rippled across the men's faces, their expressions growing as Buck's low, steady growl rumbled around the room.

Adrenaline flooded her system, growing in intensity as confusion rippled through the group. *It's their turn to wait and see what I have planned.* She put the butt of the lighter into her mouth and uncapped the bottle. Working swiftly, she took the sturdy weight of the industrial-sized bottle in hand and swung it like a bat. Clear liquid splattered over the row of men. The air was instantly thick with the pungent odor. They staggered back, more angered than concerned. That changed the moment she tossed the bottle at the center man's feet and retrieved the lighter from her mouth.

"Do any of you boys know how flammable nail polish remover is?" she asked.

One click, and a small flame danced at the tip. Her smile grew until her cheeks hurt when she saw it dawn upon them. *Step aside, or I'll light you up.*

The following seconds lingered, filled only with the sounds of Katrina's lullaby and the soft gurgle of the still-leaking jug.

"What the hell is wrong with you? Put that out!" the colossal man bellowed.

He loomed over her, his dark eyes blazing with rage as liquid dripped down his sleeve.

"Basheba," Ozzie pleaded. "We should go. We should go right now."

"What do you think I'm trying to do? These guys are blocking the way," she said.

"So you don't ask us to move?" someone she didn't bother to try to pick out of the crowd demanded. "Put the flame out, you psycho!"

Buck snarled and snapped, bracing his paws wide and lowering his skull. Basheba lowered her hand as if to drop it into the clear puddle at the men's feet.

"Your call," she said. "Move or burn."

"You threw it everywhere," a man screamed amongst a string of profanities.

"This is the only exit. The whole place will go up! You'll be trapped in here, too!"

Basheba could barely hear the man over the rising chaos behind her. The other shoppers had realized what was going on. Those who looked prepared to make a run for the door were held back by those who were terrified of her dropping the lighter.

"Are you insane?" someone screamed amongst the flood of whispered demands.

Another person called for someone to call the cops.

"I'd say it's more apathy," she commented. *Or a greater knowledge of how fires spread.* "And boredom. My arm's getting sore boys. Time to choose a side."

Life or Katrina. Which one do you love more? The men all turned to their muscled leader in the center, searching for a sign of what to do next. Wordless, the huge man took a step back. The others followed suit, parting down the center to let Basheba and Ozzie pass. Basheba kept the lighter flame burning as she strode forward. The slick liquid splashed under her hiking boots. She refused to take her eyes from the door, refused to give them any sign of weakness or fear. The men loomed over her like the battlement walls of a dark castle. As hard as she tried, she couldn't miss just how outmatched she was. Inch for inch. Muscle for muscle. Pound for pound. Buck closed in on her left side, Ozzie on her right.

With a soft beep, the automatic doors swung open and they were engulfed by the warm spring air. Her new focus became the car. And, while she let her arm drop to her side, she didn't let the lighter flick off just yet. When they were halfway to her car, she broke into a wild fit of giggles.

"What?" Ozzie asked breathlessly.

"I was so sure I was going to slip in that nail polish remover."

"You might actually be insane. Like, clinically," Ozzie said in a rush. He constantly checked over his shoulder and scanned the parking lot. "We need to leave. Now. Faster. Walk faster."

Sneaking a glance over her shoulder, she saw that, while the men now lingered by the door, none of them had moved to follow.

"We're fine."

"They called the cops," Ozzie hissed.

"So?"

"So, you threatened to burn people alive, Basheba! People who didn't do anything to us!"

"You heard the music."

"No one else did."

"They're in bed with Katrina."

"Maybe they are. What I'm asking is: how do you intend to explain any of that to an authority figure?"

"I recognize no one's authority but my own," she replied, finally letting the lighter flicker out.

A bit of his heat left his voice when she glared at him. "Okay, sure. But, the security cameras and numerous witnesses will say you went up to a group of people without warning and threatened to murder them, and courts of law exist."

Basheba opened her mouth to argue. Nothing came out. Mina and Cadwyn started to slip from the trunk to help with the groceries. Ozzie waved an arm at them, the cluster of grocery bags smacking together.

"Get in the car. We're leaving. We need to leave right now."

Clearly confused, they sank back in and awkwardly closed the hatch door. Ozzie ordered Buck in before dropping into the passenger seat, bags piled up in his lap, and almost slamming his foot in the door in his haste. The instant Basheba opened the driver's side door, Mina bombarded her with questions.

"I may or may not have done an impulsive thing," Basheba admitted.

"A crime, Basheba," Ozzie snapped, his voice increasingly inching into a squeak. "You committed a crime."

"Some people might have misjudged the situation."

"You! *You* misjudged."

Basheba clicked her tongue. "Mistakes were made."

"You threatened to set them on fire." Ozzie said each word as if it was a complete sentence.

"What is with you and fire?" Cadwyn asked casually.

She glared back at him. "What is with you and getting your butt whooped by bovines?"

"Can we leave now, please?" Ozzie pleaded, practically vibrating in his seat.

As Basheba closed the door, she noticed the sudden twist in Cadwyn's lips. His eyes were locked over her shoulder and, following his gaze, she spotted her Uncle Isaac storming toward them.

"Oh, damn it," she said in a whisper.

"Basheba!" Isaac bellowed. "We need to talk! Now!"

"I'm really getting tired of people telling me what I need to do," she mumbled before heaving a heavy sigh.

Everyone in the car stared at her, none of them voicing the questions that were clearly written on their face. Her uncle reached the edge of the parking lot and screamed for her again, ordering her out of the car.

"I'm going to have breakfast with my family," Basheba said. "Anyone want to come along?"

CHAPTER 8

Mina watched as Basheba settled down by a gravestone, resting her back against it while she munched on some dried apricots.

"This isn't exactly what I thought she was suggesting," Mina whispered to the boys, not wanting to risk her voice carrying the few feet separating them from the blonde.

Cadwyn's brow furrowed. "You thought it was more likely she would willingly be obedient to her uncle than that she'd want to eat in a cemetery? Seriously?"

Ozzie used a spork to scoop out a dollop of peanut butter and then proceeded to lick it off the spoon like a lollypop, talking around it. "Yeah, that was pretty dumb of you."

Mina turned to Cadwyn for support and only got a shrug in return. The older man offered her some salted peanuts.

"Did she get anything that's an actual breakfast food?" Mina asked, sorting through the array of bags and bottles. "Or fruit?"

"She doesn't want to eat anything from the locals," Ozzie said around his mouthful.

Heaving a sigh, Mina picked up a breakfast bar she wasn't familiar with, flipping it over to read the nutrition label.

"Wow, that's a lot of sugar."

"You know you might be murdered in the next few days," Cadwyn said.

"That doesn't mean I want to spend the rest of the time I have left feeling disgusting," she said, tossing it back into the pile.

At least the granola bar has some nutritional value, she reasoned and began picking one apart. It had to be approaching noon and the warm sunlight was heating the grass they sat upon. The air was filled with the scents of a dozen different flowers, some growing wild, and others left in remembrance for loved ones. At the top of the hill, overlooking the rustic town and surrounded by sprawling fields and woods, it was easy to forget where they were.

Only two points of destruction kept the place from looking like a postcard. The first was the funeral home, which had yet to recover from Basheba's last visit. The other was the memorial headstone for Katrina Hamilton, which had been re-erected in their absence. Basheba had kicked it back down the hill before she settled down to eat with her relatives. They were out in the open. With the high ground and a clear view of every direction. No deep shadows. No way for them to be crept up on.

Mina watched Basheba as she rested her head back against the cool, grey stone and tipped her face up to the sunlight. Buck napped with his head in Basheba's lap. The sight struck a chord in Mina. *This is the only time I've seen her relaxed.*

It made Mina think about her own family. *The flock of Cranes.*

More than two hundred smiling faces filled her mind's eye. Holidays and birthdays. Weddings and graduations. Thousands of little moments that had filled her life with warmth and companionship. An army of people ready to catch her if she fell. For the briefest moment, she tried to imagine what it would be like if every single one of them was in the ground.

"Does she really have no one?" Mina found herself asking.

Cadwyn hesitated to take a sip of his water bottle. "In the Winthrop family, we're always told to fight to the very end. Sometimes, when I look at Basheba, I think that's a stupid idea. At least the dead don't have to mourn."

"But she has to have friends?" Mina pushed. "She went to school, right?"

Cadwyn shook his head. "They were always traveling. She was homeschooled."

85

"College?"

"I don't think she ever went," Cadwyn said, chewing thoughtfully. "Hold on."

He rocked onto his side and pulled his phone out of his pocket. Wincing slightly, he sent a quick text to reassure his parents, as they all had been doing for the last hour, and started scrolling.

"What are you doing?" Ozzie asked.

"Pulling up her Instagram page," Cadwyn said, idly munching on a handful of nuts.

"Hey, we should all follow each other," Ozzie declared with a smile. "I tried to find you guys but couldn't."

"I'm *Nurse The Worst*," Cadwyn said absently. "My patients have access to the internet, so I can't use my real name. Basheba's tag is *Buck's Road Trip Adventures*."

Ozzie's enthusiasm was infectious, and they were all soon sitting with their phones. Mina wasn't surprised to find that Basheba ran her page like it was Buck's. Lots of photos of him at landmarks and tourist traps. And an admittedly cute one of him gazing lovingly at Cinderella. *Can dogs be partial to blondes?*

While there were a lot of followers, a lot of opportunity to engage with other people, Basheba didn't respond all that much. Even here she didn't want human interaction. The more she thought about it, the more Mina's sympathy became stained with fear. *She really has nothing to lose. Only Buck.* Bile splashed the back of her tongue as it sunk in. Basheba hadn't been bluffing. Not with her, not with the men at the store.

"Basheba!"

The sharp name cracked their comfortable silence. Despite his injury, Cadwyn was the first on his feet. Isaac was still at the bottom of the hill. He stormed halfway up before he noticed Cadwyn had positioned himself directly in his path, his towering form more than enough to block any view of the small girl.

"Step aside, Cadwyn. This is between me and my niece."

Mina looked between the two men. It was hard to think that the short twig with wire-rimmed glasses was any kind of threat to Cadwyn. *I bet people think that about Basheba, too.* Mina's gaze traced the thin scar that crossed Isaac's face, the one Basheba had left behind only a few months ago. Not completely healed, it was still puckered and red, and promised to be a dull grayish-white in the future. *That's never going away.* Mina thought. *You'd think it would be enough of a warning to keep your distance.*

"Isaac," Cadwyn sighed. "Just walk away."

"You're protecting her? Do you know what she did just now? She's going to ruin everything!"

"I'm protecting you," Cadwyn cut in. "She's not in the mood to tolerate you right now."

"I can handle my niece."

"There's some evidence that you can't," Ozzie said, shyly wiggling his fingers in front of his face.

Rage made Isaac's face redden, highlighting the scar all the more.

"This doesn't concern you," Isaac spat out.

"May I point something out?" Mina didn't wait for him to reply before continuing. "Basheba has proven in the past that she's willing to be violent with you. Are you sure you want to confront her in an isolated cemetery?"

Isaac jabbed a finger at her. "And your father sings your praises. You're no better than that ungrateful little wench."

Cadwyn shook his head in bafflement. "Did you just call her a—you know what? Never mind. Just leave. Take a breather. Give her a call once you've calmed down."

Isaac neither left nor came forward, just lingered there at the base of the hill, glaring at them each in turn, clearly trying to decide his next course of action.

"I'll be calling your father, too," he snarled at Cadwyn.

"I'm in my thirties, but okay."

Buck was the one that ended the stand-off. The dog emerged from behind a tombstone like a hellhound, head low, eyes fixed on him, fangs flashing as a deep threatening growl rumbled his sides. Isaac backed up and, with a final glare, stalked off with the same intensity with which he came.

Basheba whistled, light and sharp. Instantly, Buck perked up and bound off like a puppy, leaping over the headstone to get back to Basheba's side, where he was instantly lavished with affection and praise.

Cadwyn sighed. "We should move again."

"Why?" Ozzie asked. "He left."

"To contact everyone. My dad's not going to take these newest developments well," Mina answered.

Ozzie helped them pack everything back into the bags, his forehead scrunching up every so often as he thought about something.

"What did he mean by ruin everything?"

"He buddied up to the cult a long time ago," Basheba said, swooping in to snatch up some bags and head down the hill.

The painkillers must have been wearing off because Cadwyn's pace slowed as he went down the hill. Mina lingered with him, allowing Basheba and Ozzie to pack the car. As much as she didn't want to come here, Mina now found herself reluctant to leave. It seemed as if they were always getting pushed from one place to another. *If we can't get a good footing here, how are we going to survive in the woods?*

The question hovered like a fog on her brain, dulling her perception until she was barely paying attention to anything around them. She didn't even notice the woman approaching the hill until she was nearly at their car. From a distance, she looked remarkably like Basheba. It was a difference of inches. A few in height and a few around her waist. Wearing a bright summer dress, and leaving her golden hair free to trail down her back, the stranger had embraced the Disney Princess appearance Basheba downplayed with flannel and plaid.

"Oh God, no," Cadwyn said, picking up his pace.

"What now?" Mina said.

None of this was going as she had planned.

Cadwyn arched an eyebrow. "You don't know who that is?"

"I'm now guessing it's Claudia, Basheba's cousin," she said, giving him her arm to lean on as he developed a heavy limp. "Any chance she likes her more than her uncle?"

Cadwyn only laughed.

"That's not a good sign," Mina mumbled.

If she hadn't personally seen what the small woman could do when unleashed in the forest, Mina would have cut her loose by now. She was starting to hate that, despite everything, Basheba was still worth keeping around.

The ground leveled out and Cadwyn was able to move a bit quicker. They were still too late to intercept Claudia before she gained Basheba's attention. *At least she has the common sense to stay out of arm's reach*, Mina noted. They couldn't have been more than a few sentences into their conversation and already Basheba's face had settled into a neutral expression. *Another warning sign.*

"Hi," Mina cut in with a cheerful smile. "I don't think we've been introduced. I'm Mina Crane."

"Yes, of course." Claudia's smile lit up her round face, making her look all the kinder. "I'm so sorry I didn't get to meet you before. I wanted to thank you for helping my cousin. You could never know how much it means to me."

"I'm her shield," Basheba said. "As long as I'm alive, she's got less chance of getting an invite from Katrina."

Claudia flinched. "Must you call her by name?"

"Yep," Basheba chirped.

"And you know I love you," Claudia pressed on, as if Basheba hadn't spoken.

Basheba rolled her good eye. "Shows."

"It hurts me when you talk like that."

"Good."

Claudia jolted, fine lines creasing the skin between her eyes.

"They're insults, Claud," Basheba said with frustration. "I am intentionally insulting you. For the sole purpose of hurting you. How do you not get that by now?"

The larger blonde shook her head, already looking close to tears. "Don't you ever get tired of being so hateful?"

"No," Basheba smiled happily. "I find it pretty fun."

"Everyone needs their hobbies, I suppose." Claudia's voice remained kind and as gentle as a summer breeze. But Mina noticed that her watering eyes had suddenly gone dry. *She might have a bit more in common with Basheba than her father*. The idea alone scared Mina.

"Daddy is still upset about the way you treated him."

Basheba looked close to gagging. "Could you not call him that? It's so gross."

"You called Uncle Jonathan 'daddy.'"

"Couple of things," Basheba said, bracing one hand against the car as her mouth pulled tight. "Firstly, I was little. Secondly, my dad wasn't a humanoid-shaped pile of fecal matter that just *Frosty the Snowman'd* his way into consciousness. And third, you mention my dad again and this interaction is going to get real ugly, *real* quick."

"Violence is not always the answer," Claudia said.

Basheba shrugged one shoulder. "But it's always an option."

"Perhaps it would be best to get to the point," Cadwyn cut in, adding in a lighter but pinched tone. "We're all a little tense."

"Yes, of course," Claudia smiled. Puffing herself up with a deep breath, she reluctantly turned back to her cousin. "While I love you, your unscheduled visit is causing problems for a lot of people."

Mina watched the smile spread across Basheba's face and knew the girl couldn't have said anything worse.

"Aw, you're so sweet," Basheba said.

Claudia shifted her weight from one foot to the other. "You need to leave. Today, preferably."

Basheba burst into a stream of giggles. "Are you trying to run me out of town? You? Yeah, Buck should be scared of a squirrel."

"What are you even trying to achieve?" Claudia snapped, her arms flying wide and her mask of gentle perfection slipping.

"Mina wants to kill Katrina. And, you know me, I'm always up for a witch hunt."

A variety of emotions flitted across Claudia's face. All the while, her mouth hung open and her arms fell limply to her side.

"What?"

"We're going to kill Katrina."

So much for keeping a low profile, Mina thought. *Although, I guess that idea was destroyed a while back.*

"You can't do that." Claudia cleared her throat and continued. "You can't kill a ghost."

"Call it an exorcism, then."

"You can't."

Basheba giggled. "Oh, you're worried. Afraid your daddy's cult isn't going to take it well."

"Lord in heaven, Basheba, there is no cult! You and your conspiracy theories. You can't spend your whole life hunting Bigfoot and aliens."

"Watch me."

"Aliens?" Ozzie perked up.

"She used to force us all to sit outside for hours searching for UFOs," Claudia said. "Uncle Jon—"

She didn't get the whole name out before Basheba's fist cracked into her jaw. The tiny girl leaped to do it, throwing her whole weight into the blow, somehow summoning enough strength to force Claudia to the ground.

"Say his name again," Basheba hissed, her eyes full of burning fury. "I dare you."

Claudia cupped her jaw, her eyes wide and lined with pained tears. Thin trails of blood trickled from the corner of her mouth to drip into her golden hair.

"Let me look," Mina said, moving to crouch down beside the struck woman.

"Don't touch me," Claudia snapped.

She lurched onto her feet, using the few inches she had to tower over her smaller cousin.

"How dare you."

"Oh, go cry to your daddy," Basheba dismissed. Her eyes lit up as something occurred to her. "And tell him something for me, would you?"

Claudia kept her silence, her hand still protectively covering her reddening cheek.

"I thought he'd get this on his own, you know, like a sane person. But it looks like he hasn't. So, let me make this clear." Basheba took a step closer to her relative, Buck close at her heels. Despite being physically tiny, Basheba appeared to be the biggest threat. "I was *never* afraid of him. I kept my silence to protect my father. To spare him from knowing what kind of man his brother was. Now, dad's gone. And there's nothing left to protect him from me."

"What are you talking about?" Claudia whispered. "Daddy never did anything to you."

Basheba laughed, bitter and cold. "How can you function being this stupid? Just repeat that word for word to him, okay? You've pushed me too far. Come near me again, and I'll show you exactly what I did to the others."

Shoving Claudia hard in the chest, Basheba turned on her heel and stalked toward the driver's seat. Before Mina could make sense of what had just happened, Cadwyn was already steering her toward the back of the car. Claudia watched them drive away, confusion mixed with fear on her face as she hugged herself tight.

CHAPTER 9

The day passed slowly as they sat crowded in the boys' room. The beds were smaller, but there were two of them. And, since Basheba only traveled with one backpack, it was easier for the girls to move. The idea of fleeing the town while they still could had swirled amongst the group. The Witch knew they were here and Basheba's paranoia of the supposed cult had spread to Ozzie.

Everyone was on edge. No one felt in control anymore. Mina couldn't have been more surprised that Basheba had backed her up in her argument to stay. The element of surprise wasn't ever in their favor anyway. They had to be on their guard, but little had changed. If anything, Mina took this as a sign that The Witch was concerned. *Why else try to scare us off?* She couldn't shake that it was all hopeful thinking.

With the girls resolved to stay, there was no chance that Cadwyn was going to leave them. He didn't have it in his nature. Ozzie hadn't spoken much during the discussion and had simply gone along with the decision of the group. It left Mina feeling a little guilty. He was so young. She couldn't shake the idea they were manipulating him. *He shouldn't be here at all.*

They had briefly discussed heading into the woods now, escape the town, and whatever The Witch had planned next. That had died the moment Basheba shook her head. "There's not enough daylight left to get past it," Basheba had said. No one had the guts to ask her what 'it' was, leaving her to continue.

"We're better off getting as much sleep as possible and setting out at dawn".

So they had hunkered down in the bed and breakfast, all crowded into the same room, waiting for night to fall. Hours had passed slowly. Marked only by the changing light and the sporadic calls from their near frantic family members. Oddly enough, Ozzie was the best at placating them. He was always calm and collected. *His parents don't know how much danger he's in*, Mina thought as she watched him expertly turn the conversation to the dramas of some family friends.

Accustomed to long car rides, Buck didn't grow restless until the sun had dipped enough to give the light a honeyed glow. They left as a group, crowding down the narrow hallway and only pausing to let everyone use the restroom at the top of the stairs. Buck seemed to understand the shift in the air and had kept closer to his mistress than he normally would have. He had refused to even leave the porch until Basheba came down to the grass with him. Cadwyn had taken to the swinging seat, watching over Ozzie and Basheba as they played a quick game of fetch with the energized dog. Mina remained on the threshold.

The sunset painted the white apple blossoms an array of pinks, purples, and blues. The air smelled sweet and clear. Try as she might, she couldn't catch the faintest trace of a motor. No planes flew overhead. No cars rumbled down the distant road. There wasn't even a tractor to break the pristine silence.

"It's like time stopped here," Mina said.

"Yeah," Cadwyn said with a sigh. "It's ruined country getaways for me. When things get peaceful, I remember this place."

"I could see myself getting a weekend home here someday," she said, curling her fingers in the soft knit of her cardigan. "You know, if it wasn't for the murderous witch."

"She does drive down real-estate prices."

Mina smiled but she couldn't shake herself free of the melancholy that had settled into her bones. Everything about her was quaint. Beautiful. And yet, the air itself was oppressive. She felt trapped. Barely fifteen minutes had passed before they headed as a group back to the room. Mina was left unsettled by how grateful she was to retreat to their room. As a lifelong claustrophobic, small rooms had obviously never held much appeal to her. Now, it felt like safety.

Her mobile blared to life as they reached the top of the stairs and she reluctantly glanced at the screen.

"It's my dad," she said softly.

Ozzie lingered beside her as the others started down the hallway.

"Are you going to dodge him again?" he asked.

"I can't keep doing that."

Biting the inside of her cheek, she hovered her thumb over the screen, not brave enough yet to answer the call.

"Mina?" Cadwyn asked, lingering halfway between the top of the stairs and their bedroom door. "Are you coming?"

And take the call in front of Basheba? Mina thought, cringing internally.

"I'll take it in the bathroom," she said.

Ozzie straightened slightly. "Do you want me to wait?"

"No, that's okay. I'll only be a moment."

"We're not supposed to be on our own," Ozzie pressed. "I can stay outside the door. You'll have your privacy."

Cadwyn shuffled a little closer, clearly about to offer switching places with the teenage boy. Even that small movement made him wince, coaxing Mina to cut off his question before he could ask it.

"Thanks, Ozzie. I'll keep the door open a bit." She turned her smile to Cadwyn. "I'll be quick."

The older man nodded once and disappeared into the room, leaving them alone in the hallway.

"It'll be okay," Ozzie promised.

"You are so sweet," Mina said, one hand on the bathroom door handle.

He chuckled. "Just what every guy wants to hear."

"Just take the compliment," Mina said as she slipped into the room.

Alone in the bathroom, there was nothing else for her to do but

95

answer the insistent cry of her phone. She pressed the button, licked her lips, and brought the phone up to her ear.

"Hi, dad."

"That's how you start this conversation?" her father said, his voice cold and slow. "I'm sure you meant to start with an apology."

"Dad—"

"For lying to us. For running off across the country without permission. And now Isaac is calling me about this insane plan to go against The Witch. All of these you should be apologizing to me for."

Mina instantly grabbed at the one point she thought she could actually win. "I'm in college now, dad. I'm all grown up. I don't need your permission to go anywhere."

"I am your father," he snarled. "You'll never reach an age where you don't need my permission."

For a moment, she was too stunned to talk. Her father continued on in her silence.

"You're going to destroy everything Isaac worked so hard to create. Did you even think about that?"

"We've avoided his café. If he's telling you anything else, he's lying."

"I'm not talking about his pitiful little business," her father said, his voice still slow but solid. "Did you ever stop to consider how difficult it must have been for him to establish himself in that town? The truce he would have to cultivate to maintain that peace?"

Mina's stomach dropped. "Are you saying that he made a truce with The Witch?"

Basheba can't be right. Not again. Not about this.

"He's done the impossible to keep his family safe."

"He's joined up with the woman who's killed generations of his family," Mina corrected. "God, no wonder Basheba hates him. You can't come back from that kind of betrayal."

"Basheba only cares about herself. She has no idea what kind of pressure comes with being a family leader. And her refusal to breed didn't give him many choices."

"Breed?"

"Don't snap at me about semantics. When you're older, you'll see that you don't get to pick and choose which obligations to fulfill."

"No one should be forced to have children."

And she's terrified of them.

"She shouldn't have to be forced," her father said. "As a woman born into the four families, she came into the world with that burden. Ignoring it is selfish, especially when her line is dying."

"By that logic, why aren't you mad at me? I'm going to school instead of having kids. Aren't I going against the family?"

"Don't be confrontational," he signed bitterly. "You're a Crane. There're enough of us that you can have the luxury of time."

Mina stammered, "Well, while we're on the topic, I don't know if I want kids. I'm going to be busy with my career."

"We'll talk about it later," her father dismissed. Before she could press the issue, he continued, "What matters right now is that you come home before you do any more damage."

"I can't do that."

Ice entered his words. "You will, Willimina. Right now."

"Dad, I need to do this. I can do this. We can be free. You should be here helping me."

"Helping you commit suicide? You have no idea what you're dealing with."

"Because you never told me," Mina cut in, startled by the anger in her own words. "You want to talk about obligations to the family? Let's start with the fact that you keep the kids willfully ignorant."

"I tell them what they need to know."

"Stories about the Boogieman under the bed is a world away from telling them the truth about a serial killer stalking the family. They have a right to know what's coming for them. The real, brutal truth. I had a right to know."

"You're coming home, Mina."

"When I do, I'll tell them everything."

"You will keep your mouth shut!"

It was the first time in Mina's memory that she could recall her father raising his voice at her. It left her speechless.

"This is Basheba's doing. I knew she'd be a horrible influence on you," he snarled with real rage in his voice. "Mina, this is what you are going to do. You will hang up this phone and leave. I've already told Isaac to expect your arrival. He'll take you to the airport and put you on the first flight home."

"No." She could barely make the word louder than a whisper. Still, she knew he heard her because the phone line when silent.

Her hands shook as they tightened around the phone. The bathroom was too small for her to pace out her restless energy.

"I'm going to pretend I didn't hear that."

"I'm sorry, Dad, but I can't come home. Not yet. I need to do this."

"You'll die."

"Can't you just trust me?"

"Get home now, Mina."

Her heart rammed against her ribs hard enough to leave her breathless. Licking her suddenly dry lips, she stammered, "No. I'm sorry."

"You say that word to me one more time, and you won't be going to your little school anymore."

"You can't do that."

"I'm your father."

"And you don't pay my tuition. I got a free ride, I earned that."

"I pay for your rent and living expenses."

Mina froze mid-stride. "You were the one who insisted I should focus on my studies and not get a job. Was that just so you'd have something to hold over my head? Oh God, Dad. Do you hear what you're saying?"

"I hear it. I'm a father telling his wayward daughter to get back in line."

Realization settled on her mind like a branding iron. All this time, he wasn't being supportive. He wasn't proud. *He was only making sure he remained necessary to me.*

"I have to go."

"And pack your bag," he finished for her.

"Whatever you say, Dad," she said, tears pricking her eyes. Even the half-truth left a bitter taste in her mouth. "I love you."

"I love you, too. I'll see you soon."

"Yeah."

"You'll understand one day, Mina. I only ever have your best interests at heart. And I know best."

"I love you," she repeated again just to hear him repeat it back. There was a risk that she might never hear him say it again. "Goodbye."

Hanging up the phone, she braced her hands on her hips and hunched forward. Her dark hair fell around her, blocking off her view of the bathroom. A few tears dripped free as she struggled to breathe. She had never gone against her father's wishes before. *Because I've never seen this side of him before,* she reasoned to herself.

Sucking in a few deep breaths, she washed her face and raked her hands through her hair, trying to work herself back into something resembling presentable. More than once, she had to pause to collect herself. Once she was sure that she didn't look like she was on the verge of tears, she opened the door. Ozzie scrambled up onto his feet. With a soft smile, he shoved his hands into his pockets.

"Are you okay?"

"Perfectly fine," Mina said.

"You know the bathroom isn't soundproof, right?"

Mina swallowed thickly, feeling the burning lump of tears that threatened to break free.

"Don't tell Basheba any of that."

"Why would I?" he asked. "I just want to make sure you're okay."

"I'm fine," she assured. She huffed a breath and pulled a hand through her hair again. "None of this is turning out like I thought it would."

"Are you still sure we can do it?" Ozzie asked directly.

She gave it some real thought, balanced the chances, and shrugged. "Yeah. I do."

"Then I do, too," Ozzie said. "So, let's go prove it."

Warmth rimmed her eyes. Before she could overthink it, she pulled Ozzie into a tight hug.

"Thanks."

Ozzie hugged her back. "Anytime. Do you want to take a second? It's okay if you cry. It just means that you care."

Pulling back and wiping her eyes with the tips of her fingers, she smiled. "I'm good. But thanks."

"Back to the room?"

"Yeah," Mina said with a determined nod.

They turned in unison and the last flush of sunset painted the walls. Within seconds, the once dull hallway was a brilliant yellow. The buzzing started softly. Barely more than a whisper that crept from walls. It steadily grew louder, becoming a constant hum as the wallpaper began to shift and bulge. Mina's nose wrinkled at the new scent that drenched the air. *Honey.*

Ozzie latched onto her hand and tugged her forward. He didn't hesitate to break into a full out sprint. They only got a few paces before the walls began to rot. The wallpaper became brittle, flaking away in patches to create a patchwork of holes. Bees writhed within the gaps. Crawling over each other as thick honey wept from the gaping honeycomb wounds.

Mina's chest squeezed tight until she choked on her suddenly rapid breathing. Sweat prickled her hairline and she clutched tight to Ozzie's hand.

"Just keep moving," Ozzie said.

The swarm poured out of the walls. Honey drenched the floor, creating a puddle that made them fight for every step.

"It's okay, we're almost there," Ozzie assured, tugging her forward again. The buzzing increased, covering every trace of thought that crossed her mind. All she could do was follow where Ozzie led her as the world around them became a gigantic hive.

She slammed into Ozzie's back as he abruptly stopped short. Panting hard, she crowded into him and balled her free hand into the back of his shirt. Only then was she brave enough to glance over his shoulder and see what horror could compete with the nightmare around them. A dark figure stood at the other end of the hallway, with their bedroom door between them. There was barely enough room for its looming stature. But it was also broken. Its limbs hung limply, and it struggled to hold its head up, flopping it from side to side as if its neck was broken. Throwing its shoulders back, it lulled its head up so they could see its face.

"Mina," Ozzie whispered. "You see a scarecrow, too, right?"

"Yeah," she whispered.

Moving in jerking lurches, the scarecrow dragged itself free of the honey-covered floor. It crawled onto the walls. Each touch shattered the decaying honeycomb. Bees rallied against the intrusion and poured out of the gap, their numbers so large they looked like billowing smoke.

Mina's scream covered Ozzie's own. They both staggered back, trying to escape the onslaught. The scarecrow clawed faster toward them. Each touch upon the honeycomb wall released a new flood of insects. They swarmed toward them and Mina realized they were being driven back. Either to the bathroom or back out of the house.

"She's trying to separate us." The fragment of thought toppled out of her mouth.

Ozzie's eyes were wide, his breathing quick, but he tightened his grip on her hand and asked a silent question. The bees surrounded them, their stingers sinking into their flesh and creating a flash of pain that cleared her thoughts. She squeezed his hand back and they both raced forward. Into the swarm. Closer to the scarecrow. Pain exploded within every cell of her body. She couldn't hear anything beyond the never-ceasing hum.

"Basheba!" Ozzie screamed. He tried to call for Cadwyn, too, but the swarm attacked his mouth, making him choke and sputter.

His pace faltered and he tripped. Mina released the back of his shirt to wrap her arm around his waist, dragging him forward. Through the swarm, the shadow of the scarecrow clawed closer. Its fingers ripped chunks from the walls. It was racing them to the door.

"Hurry," Mina sobbed, trying to pull Ozzie back into a regular pace.

They reached the door and scrambled for the handle, barely able to see or breathe while the swarm attacked her face. "Basheba!"

The door ripped away from her hand. She didn't wait to throw herself inside, slamming down upon the floor and bringing Ozzie down with her.

"Close the door!"

It was a waste of her breath. Cadwyn had already slammed the door shut, holding it in place with his body weight.

"The box!" Mina gasped, thrusting a hand toward her backpack.

She had already crawled out from under Ozzie and staggered to her feet by the time Basheba tossed her one of the containers Mina had brought with her. With swollen fingers, she ripped the box open and staggered to the door. The bees that had invaded the room with her swarmed with renewed force. Fire burned under her skin, boiling her alive, making her hand tremble as she poured the salt in a line across the threshold. She had to shove Cadwyn's legs out of the way to complete the trail. Half of the bees attacking her decayed into dust while the last grains of salt completely covered the threshold.

"Bloody hell," Basheba mumbled, swatting at the remaining insects. She clapped her hands and Mina threw the box back to her.

In quick order, Basheba sealed the windows. Mina scrambled to her back, retrieved another box, and did the same for the fireplace.

The world fell silent. The pain ebbed away. Mina flopped down on the floor, breathing hard and resisting the urge to curl herself into the fetal position. They were gone but she could still feel them. As if they covered her. Crawling and squirming and piercing her flesh.

"I swear people have tried salt before," Cadwyn said numbly.

"It's my own blend," Mina said, pulling her aching body into a seated position. She noticed them staring at her. "I did some research on ancient European methods. Salt repels ghosts, iron wards off evil spirits, and sprigs of mistletoe were used to keep witches out of homes. I hypothesized that a mixture of all three wouldn't diminish the effectiveness of each individual component."

Basheba stared at her, jaw hanging wide. "Am I actually starting to like you?"

"I'm not sure I want that," Mina replied, a weak smile pulling at her still stinging lips.

The fragile peace shattered when the knocking started.

"Cadwyn," a soft voice whispered. "Cadwyn, open the door."

CHAPTER 10

"Cadwyn."

Years had passed since Cadwyn had last heard the voice whispering to him through the thin, wood door. Still, he recognized it instantly and it left him reeling with shock.

"Cadwyn, please. Open the door."

"Who is that?" Ozzie asked, still sprawled across the floor at Cadwyn's feet.

Staring at the door, Cadwyn tried to respond, to form the name that screamed within his skull. Nothing came out.

"Cadwyn, I'm scared. Let me in."

Long dormant instinct kicked in, forcing him to reach for the door handle without conscious thought. Basheba's small hand latched onto his wrist and stilled him. Numbly, he stared at her fingers for a long moment, not seeming to understand why his arm had stalled.

"Do not open that door," Basheba commanded.

"I have to."

"What?" she asked.

"Open the door. I'm scared," the voice whispered with urgency.

Cadwyn snapped around to the door, "Abraham."

Basheba squeezed his forearm, the nip of her nails drawing his attention back.

"Abraham died," she said, strong but gentle. "His music box opened, the demon was unleashed, and it killed him."

Tears burned his eyes, falling free as he trembled.

"I killed him," Cadwyn said. "I did that. When he couldn't take it anymore."

"That's not on you. Katrina forced him into a horrible situation. You did what you did, what you had to do, to set him free," Basheba said.

Cadwyn turned to the door, and she squeezed his arm again.

"He's dead, Cadwyn. Whatever thing that is, it's not your brother."

Swallowing thickly, he asked in a whisper. "What if death doesn't release us? What if she gets to keep the souls?"

"She doesn't," Basheba answered swiftly.

"How do you know?"

"Because if I let myself think anything different, I would go insane," Basheba said. "We die. We're free. That's it."

"Cadwyn, I'm scared."

He jerked toward the door. The short girl threw herself between him and the wood.

"She can only do cheap imitations, Cad," Basheba snapped. "And they're always messed up *Frankenstein* monstrosities. Whatever that thing out there looks like, you don't need to see it."

He didn't mean to move toward her. Or loom over her tiny frame with his shoulders squared and anger curling his lips. Cadwyn couldn't recall how he got into that position, but he found himself staring down at her with a volatile mixture of fear, rage, and pain.

"It's all I can do," he choked out. "That's how it always was. That's all I was able to do. Watch."

"You don't owe the dead anything," Basheba said.

"I owed it to him when he was alive!" Cadwyn snarled. "No matter what I did, it never let me take the focus off of him for long."

Basheba softened her tone, "It wasn't your demon to endure."

"I was the one who could take it!"

The words burst out from the depths of his soul. He could feel the damage reverberate through his bones and scrape along the underside of his skin. Holding his breath was the only way to keep himself from breaking into a fit of sobs. And still, the voice of his brother called to him, begged him, pleaded to be allowed to come inside.

"I have to see what she did to him. I just have to."

Basheba caught his arm again. "Do you want them to see it, too?"

She gestured with her free hand to Mina and Ozzie. The teenagers had backed as far away from the door as the limited space would allow. Fear still radiated from them. In their eyes and the quickened pace of their breath. The fine trembling of their hands, and the way they subconsciously clutched handfuls of the other's shirt.

"Katrina's been playing with them all day. You're going to let her go for another round?" Basheba pushed. "Go on, ask them. Let them vote on if you should open the door or not."

Cadwyn narrowed his eyes on her even as his anger slipped away.

"It's all I can do for him," he whispered.

"You've done all you can do." She stepped closer to him, her tone softening until her words almost flowed like a lullaby. "He fought as hard as he could for as long as he could, and now he gets to rest. You do, too. If you let her do this to you, she wins. I'm not going to let Katrina win another round."

The barest hint of a threat weaved its way into the last sentence. Cadwyn didn't question how far Basheba would go to 'win.' It didn't matter. All of his focus was on the teenagers that had, in turn, seen too much, and nowhere near enough. It ripped him apart, but he let his arm drop.

"Cadwyn?" The voice called.

Balling his hands, he lowered his head, riding out the crushing waves of guilt and terror that raged within him. *I'm not betraying him. I'm not leaving him alone. He's gone. I have to protect the living.*

"Cadwyn, please. Don't leave me with her. I don't want to die alone."

Cadwyn squeezed his eyes tight, feeling a few tears slip free. "He didn't. I made sure he didn't."

Silence was his response. Basheba slipped her hand to the middle of his back and pushed him forward.

"Go hug Buck. He makes everything better," she said.

"Cadwyn? Cadwyn! Let me in!"

The door shook violently as something large slammed against it. Clawing and scratching and screaming with wild fury. Abraham's voice cracked as he howled, twisted up with something dark and primal until the sound alone left ice in his veins.

"You coward," it snarled like a feral beast. "You swine. You murdered him, Cadwyn. Tell yourself whatever you want, but you butchered your brother."

Slowly, he twisted around to face the door.

"Cadwyn?" Basheba said slowly.

"I know that voice," he whispered. "It's the same demon."

It can't be. It's not the Harvest season. He had always been taught that Katrina's demon could only walk the earth during Katrina's Harvest. A few days in October, that's all they were supposed to get.

"None of the music boxes opened," Cadwyn whispered to Basheba. "It shouldn't be here. It shouldn't be able to be here."

"Oh, I never left," the demon purred in its militated voice. "I couldn't go without you, Cadwyn."

"Hey, Mina, I don't suppose you brought earplugs," Basheba called out.

"I saw you in the forest," the demon continued. "I was so sad we didn't have time to play together again. Don't you worry, Cadwyn. We will. We'll have days together. I promise you that. Make it easier on yourself. Let me in."

"Go back to hell," Cadwyn snarled.

Cracks riddled the door as the demon pounded against it again, more violent than before. It ranted and raged, spewing out profanities and weaving elaborate tales of things it would do to them once it got inside. Cadwyn staggered back from the door, absently reaching for Basheba for some human contact. Something to ground him and reassure him that he was okay, that he was safe. That he wasn't back to being a skinny twelve-year-old boy alone in a cheap hotel with his brother and the demon that tortured them both. Basheba latched onto his hand and squeezed it.

"Did you get dentures, Cadwyn? Or did they find a way to root those fake chunks into your gums? I hope it's the gums. I want to rip them out again, one by one. Do you remember the pliers, Cadwyn? Do you remember the way you screamed?"

Basheba squeezed his hand until pain shot up from his palm. It grounded him in the here and now. *I'm not a kid anymore. I'm not alone.*

"I remember what you did," Cadwyn called out. "Do you remember me sending you back to where you came from?"

The taunt brought more fury than Cadwyn had expected. The walls rattled with the blows.

"Now, I'm back. And I want your teeth. I'll get them when I rip that tongue of yours right out of your mouth!"

Plaster rained down upon them from the cracking ceiling.

"I'm coming for you, Cadwyn! I'm going to get you! You never escaped me! You never will!"

Cadwyn's whole body began to shake. Childhood fears and the terrors that still lingered in his nightmares crushed down upon him. He crumbled under the weight of it, but the attack didn't stop. An onslaught of grotesque desires filled the air, screamed out by a thousand voices until everything else faded away.

Basheba tugged hard on his arm, making him stumble forward. He couldn't recall when he had started crying, but he wasn't sure if he could stop. She shoved him onto one of the beds and searched through her bag.

The building shook around them, adding to the falling dust. He looked up, worried the old structure wouldn't hold, and jumped when Basheba shoved a set of headphones onto his ears. Even at its highest volume, Basheba's mobile phone couldn't drown out the screaming demon, but it dulled the other sounds. Made them manageable.

He sucked in a deep breath, vaguely aware of the two teens crawling into bed beside him. They followed Basheba's example, each pulling out their own mobiles and pumping music into their ears. Seeing them tremble with terror forced him to focus. There wasn't much he could do. No escape. *Don't force them to watch,* a voice whispered in the back of his head. He got up and, with one long stretch of his body, he snatched up the comforter from the other bed.

Ozzie and Mina curled up against his left. Basheba and Buck crammed themselves onto what little space remained on his right. Cadwyn settled the blanket over them, creating a dim cave that cut them off from the rest of the room. The dust still fell. The door still barely stood against the onslaught. And the demon still screamed from only a few feet away. But they no longer had to see it. *We can wait it out,* Cadwyn told himself, cradling the teenagers closer. *Katrina's never had the stamina. The demon can't get in.* He squeezed his eyes shut and focused on the pounding beat of the music. *We can wait them out.*

***

It took Ozzie a while to master how to leave it all behind. His flesh, the noise, everything that his reality had become. Focusing on the music allowed him to slip away, to drift within his skull on the tide of music and rhythmic beats. A small ping jerked him back into his own skin. Sitting up made both Cadwyn and Mina stir. They both sent questioning looks at him, exhaustion and fear clear on their faces. Ozzie checked his phone and held it up for them to see the 'low battery' warning.

Slipping off the bed to get his charger, he almost fell flat on his face. Hours must have passed since they had huddled under the blanket and he had moved little since then. His muscles protested the motion to the point that they felt as if they were snapping apart under his skin. He ended up lunging out of the bed. After hours in the confined space, the night air hit him with an icy chill. Dust billowed up with every step he took, choking the air and diffusing the moonlight into a misty haze. Instantly, he wanted to climb back under the blanket. *I could just listen for a while. How bad could it be?* Then he spotted Cadwyn peeking out from under the blanket to watch him and he steeled his spine.

He knew Cadwyn wouldn't think any less of him if he showed his fear. Somehow, that made him want to hide it all the more. Cadwyn had been the one to see Ozzie fall apart in the woods. Had held him tight and told him it was okay to cry. *Let her break you. And build yourself into something stronger with the rubble.* Cadwyn's words rolled around his head, and Ozzie forced himself to give a reassuring smile. Knowing he couldn't hold it for long, he turned his back to search through his backpack.

It was moments like these that Ozzie found the hardest to deal with. Adrenaline saw him through the attacks. The need to attack or, at least, react kept his mind occupied. But when there was nothing left to do except wait, Ozzie felt as if his skin was crawling over his bones. He couldn't keep his hands from shaking. A thousand 'what ifs' battled with the exhaustion that came with his adrenaline crash.

Finally finding the charger cord and adapter, he straightened and began his search for an outlet. Cadwyn slid one hand out from under the blanket and pointed to the lamp on the bedside table. It took Ozzie a moment to realize that he was telling him to follow the lamp's cord to find it. *Right. Logic.* Mentally kicking himself for being so stupid, Ozzie crawled over the foot of the bed. He didn't want to go near the door if he didn't have to.

Scrambling ungracefully with locked muscles, he made it to the far side of the bed, then froze solid. Childhood fears of monsters lurking under the bed bubbled up from the forgotten recesses of his mind. A part of him didn't want to look. Didn't want anyone in the room to see him give in to such childish fears. *They already think of you as the baby.*

In that moment, all the extravagance of his sixteenth birthday felt ridiculous. His parents had played up the importance of the age, as if being sixteen made him more of an adult than he was at fifteen. It all felt absurd now. No one considered him any more competent than they had before. *Just put your feet on the floor and walk.*

Still, he couldn't bring himself to do it. *There are real monsters in the house. It's not stupid to check a logical and accessible hiding place. What if they can come up through the floor?* By the time he had finished his pep talk, he truly believed that something was hiding just below the mattress. Slowly, he let his arms lower himself down and lay flat upon the end of the bed. He didn't know when each tremble of the building had stopped releasing new dustings of plaster. All he knew was the air felt cold and almost solid against this spine.

Tipping over the edge of the mattress, he noticed the comforter had fallen to brush against the floorboards, effectively blocking him from seeing anything that might be waiting for him. Carefully, he began to gather up the length of material. Inch by inch. Like if he moved slow enough he might not disturb the lurking monster. Once it was done, he slid forward, took in a sobering breath, and tipped forward. All of the images he had created in his mind faded in a flash of reality. *Nothing.* Just the floorboards and a couple of dust bunnies.

The tension that had wrapped around him snapped, leaving him to sag forward. *Idiot. I'm such an idiot.* Not brave enough to look up and see Cadwyn's gentle, encouraging smile. Without looking, he knew the older man would already be peeking out over the top of the blankets to keep an eye on him. Ozzie crawled off the bed and went in search of the outlet. It was in this last bit of motion that he accidentally knocked the lump that was Buck. He grumbled his protest but seemed to give up halfway through and went back to sleep.

Wish I was him, Ozzie thought.

Once more, he stopped abruptly. Basheba was curled up on the very edge of the bed. Dust coated blonde hair fell across her face in streaks, stirring slightly as she breathed. *Is she asleep?* Against himself, he checked with Cadwyn, as if the older man could make sense of how the only one amongst them without headphones had managed to nod off. Cadwyn followed his gaze and grinned, the blankets covering his broad shoulders jostling slightly with his barely contained chuckling. *Yeah, she's asleep.*

A few moments of silence separated the songs on his phone. In those seconds, he was exposed to the full weight of the demon's perverse words. *At least it's not screaming anymore,* Ozzie thought, trying to make his own words loud enough within his skull to drown out everything else. The relief that came with the new song renewed his focus to find the outlet.

Moving silently so as not to wake Basheba, he found the lamp's cord and followed it to the wall outlet. It was situated under the window, giving him something to balance against as he squatted down, his muscles screaming as they stretched. Eventually, he was able to fumble everything into place and his phone began to charge. Only once everything was in place and he had struggled his way back up into a standing position, did he realize he was now, essentially, tied to the wall.

For the briefest moment, he eyed Basheba, wondering if he could get away with nudging her out of the way. Cadwyn seemed to read his mind and arched an eyebrow. Somehow, that tiny motion carried a complete message. *Remember how she's not a morning person?* Ozzie pressed his lips tightly together and nodded swiftly. *Bad idea. At least I'll be able to stretch out my legs a bit.*

Really, he didn't want to. He wanted to crawl back into the bed with everyone else and try to forget about everything. To seek out the comfort and safety of the group. For all of that, he was too afraid to face the world without the shield of his music. So he waited. Nervously stretching out his legs and searching for anything to keep his mind occupied. Bit by bit, his phone began to charge, and he found himself gazing out of the window. The night was thick and heavy. A shroud of velvet ebony that allowed the town to glow in the distance and the stars to shine like a stream of diamonds.

He looked out over the orchard. Drenched in the moonlight, the trees almost looked like clouds. If he tried, he could imagine he was flying. Ozzie almost smiled at the thought. The decision to learn how to fly had been a result of his last encounter with the Witch. He had yearned for something to help him feel in control again. Something he could master and hold before him as proof that he was better than he had been before. Stronger in some way. He had wanted to prove to his parents that he was okay. To Percival, his biological father, that he could make a good Sewall. And, to Cadwyn, that he had managed to make something worthwhile out of the rubble the Witch had left him as. *It seems kind of stupid now,* he thought. *Wilderness survival would have been smart. Maybe something physical, like parkour. How long does it take to master jumping across rooftops?*

His thoughts were disrupted by a flicker of light. It came and faded so swiftly, he doubted he had seen it. Leaning closer to the glass, he peered into the shadows, tracing the lines and curves of the thick orchard trees. Another flash of light forced him even nearer to the window till the tip of his nose pressed against the warmed glass. Two points of burning light trailed across the horizon, flickering as it passed through the foliage, steadily growing larger and multiplying. Ozzie frowned as the small orbs became a long trail.

Silence cracked down upon them, heavy and complete, thickening the air more than the lingering floating dust did. Ozzie leaped back from the window, his earbuds ripping free to clatter against the wall. Near frantic, he reached over and shook the bedpost, hissing at the others to wake up. Cadwyn and Mina bolted upright. It seemed to be their sudden movement more than anything else that woke both Basheba and Buck.

"What's going on?" Basheba grumbled.

"We don't know," Mina whispered.

The blonde snatched up a pillow and, after thumping it a few times, flopped down upon it. "Wake me when there's something for me to stab."

"Um, guys," Ozzie said. He didn't know why he kept his voice low, but he couldn't seem to raise it much louder than Mina's whisper. "There might be something going on outside."

"Like what?" Mina asked.

"Ghost orbs, maybe?"

Even wounded, Cadwyn's long limbs allowed him to easily climb over Basheba. He limped slightly as he rushed to Ozzie's side. By the time Ozzie turned back to the window, the floating fireballs had emerged from the darkness. *Not ghost orbs,* Ozzie thought with a sinking dread.

The wide expanse of the front yard was filled with people. They strode toward the house, flaming torches held high above their heads, eyes fixed upon the house. Ozzie's breath caught in his throat as he noticed the huge man from the supermarket leading the charge. Cadwyn and Mina crowded around him to stare out the window.

"Hey, Basheba," Cadwyn called.

"Napping," Basheba grumbled.

"Basheba. Up. Now."

Grudgingly, she flopped the blankets back and sat up. "If all of this is just to give that drama queen Katrina more attention—"

"There's an angry mob on the front yard," Mina cut in.

"The cult?" Basheba kicked the blankets the rest of the way off of her legs.

"And you might get to stab someone," Ozzie said numbly, pointing down at the man now standing next to the living mountain. "Isn't that your uncle?"

CHAPTER 11

Basheba's boots shielded her feet from the chilly floorboards. Stifling a yawn, she padded over to join the others, adjusting her eyepatch as she went. *Sleeping with it on isn't a good idea.* She barely remembered to keep to the shadows. Tomorrow would be the full moon and the plump disc was already emitting a startling amount of light. Grudgingly, Basheba had to admit that the timing had been a good choice on Mina's part. There wasn't anything worse than being in the Witch Woods during a new moon. After a few groggy blinks, Basheba realized the light was growing. *Firelight,* she thought, her interest pricked. She half-slumped against the wall and craned her neck to glance outside. A sea of burning torches steadily seeped from the shadows to pool on the front lawn.

As they watched, their numbers grew, allowing the combined glow of the flames to illuminate their faces. The stark contrast of light and shadow rendered them almost unidentifiable. Still, it barely took more than a glance to find her spindly uncle amongst the larger locals. *So this is the cult.* Seeing them all set out before her, she realized she should have been able to pick them out of the general crowd long ago. *It's all about the excess.* Everyone before them was weighed down by either extra fat or muscle.

"Livestock," Basheba whispered, the last traces of sleep draining away.

"What did you say?" Mina asked.

Basheba jerked her chin to gesture to the crowd below. "Don't they look like livestock to you? Slaughter-ready hogs and prized draft horses. Here I thought Katrina would consider her cult a, well, cult. I forgot how proud she was of her livestock. She never stopped cultivating her animals. She just switched species."

"They're a mob," Mina whispered. "But we have no proof they're a cult."

"They look kinda cult-ish," Ozzie commented, his voice softer than the others as he skittishly eyed the crowd. "But shouldn't they be wearing masks or something?"

Basheba eyed the teenager from the corner of her eyes, not quite sure if he was serious. "They plan on murdering us all."

Ozzie cringed back from the window.

"Livestock," Cadwyn pondered. "That makes sense." He elaborated once he noticed the looks Mina and Ozzie were giving him. "Her slaves? Honestly, how watered down is the history they taught you? A vast amount of the Witch's wealth came not from the land, but from the slaves she, for lack of a better word, bred. Hers were renowned for being obedient and strong."

"I thought she was impoverished and that's what started this all," Ozzie said. "When she had to sell off her property to the Bell family, and got jealous that they knew how to make the land work."

Cadwyn's eyes flicked restlessly, trying to get an idea of just how badly they were outnumbered. "Black River had a smallpox outbreak about five years before the Bells arrived."

"A highly infectious disease in cramped slave quarters?" Mina looked sickened and sorrowful at the thought. "They never stood a chance."

"The financial hit was why she had to sell the property to the Bells," Cadwyn concluded. Abruptly, he snapped his face down to frown at the youngest two. "I'm sorry, this is bothering me. Are you saying that no one ever mentioned to either of you that the Witch was a slave master?"

"My family's stories kept more to what happened after her death," Mina admitted. "I'm only starting to realize just how much they've been keeping from me."

"You're only getting that now?" Basheba scoffed as she returned to the bed to retrieve her backpack. "You're such a slow learner."

"As long as I learn," Mina said, her eyes narrowing with annoyance.

Basheba could only shrug at that, a reaction the teenager obviously wasn't expecting and didn't know what to do with. Which only made the whole thing more satisfying on Basheba's end.

"Is anyone else worried that Mina's salt mixture doesn't actually work?" Ozzie asked. "I mean, what if the demon could get in this whole time but it didn't really try to? What if it just wanted to make sure we didn't get out? Not until they came."

Basheba's gut gave a painful squeeze. Her motions slowed as she caught Cadwyn's eyes. "Boy's got a point."

She let the others discuss the matter in dreaded whispers while she pulled out her collars. It had long since become an unofficial tradition to wear them during the Harvest sacrifices. Thick, leather bands, studded with sharpened, metal spikes, polished to a high sheen that shone like quicksilver in the weakest light.

Fastening the collar first, she then worked on the cuffs as she mentioned to the still arguing group, "Is someone keeping an eye on the cult?"

"Right," Ozzie stammered.

As the one closest to the window, he took sentry point. "There's more of them."

"How many?" Basheba asked, tossing the drawstring bag that held the other cuffs and collars at Cadwyn's feet.

It landed with a loud clatter of metal. Ozzie counted in a soft murmur.

"About twenty."

"About?" Mina asked, working on her collar.

"It's dark down there. I can't tell if anyone's lurking in the trees."

Basheba called Buck over to her. He grumbled while getting out from under the warmed blankets, pausing to stretch and release a jaw-cracking yawn.

"I know, buddy," Basheba cooed. "They always pick the worst times to try and kill us."

When she had decided to attend the Medieval Fair, she had only been looking to see some guys on horseback slamming into each other. Discovering a man who created custom body armor for dogs was a special delight. It had cost her a small fortune, but it was worth it. Knowing Buck was protected was worth any price. He took the weight of the metal scales like it was nothing. Getting the helmet on was always the hardest part. He wouldn't stop trying to lick her face and chew the straps.

"There," she said, rocking back onto her heels. "Such a handsome boy. You ready to raise some hell?"

He barked once and plopped his rump on the ground.

"Um, Basheba," Ozzie said. "Your uncle is talking to that big guy from the store."

"I knew it," she chimed before standing up and walking over.

When she took Ozzie's position, he awkwardly backed up, letting Cadwyn put the last collar on him. She studied the group.

"Yeah, that's too many people. We need to lure them into the woods."

Mina jerked. "The woods?"

"I saw a demon waiting for us on the other side of the bull's paddock," Cadwyn said.

"There's one waiting outside the door," Basheba countered. "And a cult down there. At least in the woods, we'd only have the demon to deal with."

"Unless they follow," Mina said.

"They won't," Basheba said. "No locals ever go into the Witch Woods. Their loyalty to Katrina doesn't give them safety in her home. Either they'll stop following us, or I'll have an eventful evening with considerably fewer participants."

"That's quite an assumption," Mina noted.

Basheba heaved a sigh and held her arms out to better display her tiny stature. "I operate by killer doll rules, okay? My upper body strength is a joke and most people can drop kick me. In a one-on-one fight, I'm useless. But give me some guerilla warfare tactics and the element of surprise, and I'm lethal."

Mina stared at her for a moment before realization dawned on her and her jaw dropped.

"They're human," Mina said.

"We know," Ozzie said in confusion.

Mina ignored him. "We're not killing them."

"I doubt you'll be doing much of anything useful," Basheba countered.

"Basheba?" Ozzie asked in a squeak.

She sighed, fighting back the first traces of guilt. "Do any of you actually believe we're going to get out of this situation without bloodshed?"

"But," Ozzie stammered, finally catching on. "They're human."

"Don't worry about it," Basheba dismissed. "I'll do all the heavy lifting. Just like always. All you have to do is get your stuff and make sure you're ready to run."

"We'll cut through the bull's pen; create a bit more chaos for them to pursue us," Cadwyn said.

Basheba paused for a moment and eyed him carefully. "Are you okay to run?"

"Give me a minute to take another dose of painkillers before you make things worse?"

"You better hurry," she smirked. "I've been struck with the sudden urge to make life utterly unbearable for people."

With practiced ease, he administered the shot and finished getting the others in order, making sure they weren't about to leave anything valuable behind.

"So, what do you plan we do for the distraction?" Ozzie asked, pulling the strap of his bag higher onto his shoulder.

"Haven't decided yet."

Mulling their limited options over wasn't any help. Long-set plans weren't exactly in her wheelhouse. *That's more Mina's thing*, she decided as she jumped up onto the narrow window ledge. There was just enough room for her to stand upright, and she kept on her toes to make sure she didn't disturb the line of salt. Unhooking the metal latch and ignoring the questions from the others, she swung the window open wide.

"Hey, Uncle!" She leaned back against the window frame and beamed down at the crowd. "Did Claudia pass along my message?"

Isaac stopped talking to the bull-man and tipped his head back to glare up at her. "Yes, she did."

"Surprised to see you here, then. Didn't think you'd have the guts to be in the same state as me."

"Look around you, Basheba. You don't seem all that threatening at the moment. Surrounded. Scared. With the use of only one eye."

She let all the venom she felt for the man seep into her smile. "And I could lose a lot more and still be more competent than you. We're going to have to have a long talk once this is over."

"You're only getting through this night with my help," Isaac sneered. "I'm here to try and save you."

"From what? The walking fire hazard?" She turned her smile to the bull-man. "I hope you boys washed up properly. I'd hate for a stray ember to light you up like a Roman candle."

The bull-man's face scrunched up with sharpened rage. "You're not welcome here."

His voice effortlessly boomed through the still night air.

"Yeah," Basheba shrugged. "I've been picking up on that vibe. You guys are always so subtle."

"Must you antagonize them?" Mina whispered harshly.

Basheba scrunched up her eyebrows. "What did you think I was going to do?"

"Maybe not get us killed," Mina said.

After a snort, Basheba returned her attention back to the mob.

"Okay, let's move this along. Hit me with it," she called down to them.

The bull-man frowned. "Excuse me?"

"I'm sure you practiced it in your head all the way over here, just to make sure that it sounds appropriately scary. So, let me hear it."

The man's brow furrowed, and, for a moment, it almost looked like he was going to check with Isaac to see if she was serious.

"Oh, don't be shy! I'm sure it's great!" She crossed her arms over her chest, lifting one hand to roll a wrist while adding. "It's going to be stereotypical as hell, but that's fine."

"What is wrong with you?" Isaac snapped.

"What? He's undoubtedly got an evil-guy threatening speech. Watch, I'm calling it now. His spiel is going to contain a reference to Katrina, something about the greater good, and a general threat to my person."

"Do you think your petulance will save you?" the bull-man bellowed.

"No, I think a vast amount of violence will do that," Basheba smiled.

The air shifted against Basheba's back as Cadwyn slipped a little closer. "Are you sure about this?"

"I'm halfway to certain," she whispered back, her mind still skipping over their dwindling options.

At least the morons are keeping to the front, she thought. Although there was no way to tell how many people were circling around the back, she was relatively sure her blatant disregard for the situation was enough to distract them, keep them pooled together instead of spreading out. *We need to speed this up. Force them to make their move before they're ready.* There was only one way she knew to force someone to bite. And that was to get them too blind with rage to think clearly.

"You brought this upon yourself," the man continued, his voice solid enough to invade the room and roll off the walls. "Did you honestly think you could invade the Witch's territory and not have her retaliate?"

"Oh my God. Seriously? You guys can't even call her by her name?" Basheba shouted down. "How does it feel to be her pet?"

"You've angered her. All that you have done has put the entire town at risk of her vengeance."

"Is that covered by your homeowner's insurance?" Basheba said, adding for good measure, "I'm curious. When you knew you'd have to form a cult and get on board with human sacrifices to appease a long-dead witch, how did you not think, 'maybe I'll move?'"

The taunting worked enough that the man began to seethe. He glared up at her, his beefy hands clenching hard enough to make his arm tremble. *Come on, just be stupid already.*

"Come out here now. Meet your doom, and we'll let the others live."

"Bingo!" Basheba declared, throwing her arms in the air and cheering.

"This is serious, Basheba," Isaac snapped. "What are you playing at?"

"Oh, hey! I got Bingo!" Basheba declared, counting it off on her fingers. "Katrina namedrop, mentioning the greater good, and a personal threat. And in only a few sentences, too. What do I win?"

"You will die screaming!" the bull-man roared.

"And you're going to die tonight," she countered, a large, victorious smile stretching her lips wide.

It was that expression, she knew, that finally broke the man below her. His hand clutched the base of his flaming torch until the wood crackled apart. Moving as a mound of trembling fury, he surged to the front door and out of sight, leaving the confused crowd behind him.

"About damn time," Basheba muttered to herself as she leaped down from the ledge. "Okay, guys. Here's the game plan. Lock the door after me and be ready to run when I—" The sentence stumbled to a stop on her tongue as she realized she still hadn't settled on a plan. "When I do whatever it is that I'm going to do."

"That man's going to get into the house," Ozzie stammered, his eyes wide with fear.

"That was the plan," Basheba said. "I need at least one of them."

She checked that her hunting knife was still securely strapped to her lower back and grabbed one of the salt boxes for good measure.

"You can't go out there alone," Ozzie insisted.

"I won't be. I'll have Buck."

Her dog perked up at the mention of his name and he began to wriggle with anticipation.

"What do you intend to do?" Cadwyn asked, eyeing her with suspicion.

Basheba shrugged, "Don't worry about it."

"How are we supposed to know when to run in when we don't know what you're doing?" Mina asked.

"Don't worry. I'll make it so obvious that even you won't miss it."

During the conversation, Basheba had retrieved a reusable plastic bag from her backpack, dumping the hair ties it contained into the depths of her bag and refilling it with a bunch of the salt mixture. She nuzzled the open end under the door and reached for the handle. Ozzie stopped her.

"Time is a factor here, buddy," she chirped.

"I want to help you," Ozzie said. "I want to come with you."

A giggle left her mouth before she realized the boy was serious. Cringing slightly at the teenager's embarrassment, she schooled her features and tried to salvage his pride.

"My grandma used to say, 'there are times when we need violent people to do wicked things.'" She paused to glance around the room. "And, since I'm the only naturally violent person here, this stuff is kind of my responsibility. Not yours. Not Cadwyn's. Not Mina's." She smiled at him brightly and knocked her knuckles against his shoulder. "Step off my turf, Sewall."

"But—"

"The best way you can help me is to do what Cadwyn tells you to do, and stay out of my way." Before he could argue, she slipped closer to him and whispered. "There's going to be blood. Probably a lot of it."

As hard as he battled to keep his determined expression, he couldn't hide the way his face paled at just the mention of it. Below them, the door crashed against the wall, announcing that someone had entered the house.

"Okay, Buck." She beamed at the Rottweiler, her attention alone enough to make him grumble and squirm with barely contained delight. "You got your war face on?"

Reaching behind her back, she pulled her hunting knife free and raised her foot. In that moment, reality became merely a suggestion on the outskirts of her awareness. Everything inconsequential fell away, allowing her focus to narrow on the course she had set herself. All that mattered now was the dog by her side, the weight of the knife in hand, and the mysteries lurking on the other side of the door.

"Ya ready, boy?"

He yelped and nosed at the doorjamb, scratching at it hard enough to peel away the paint. Settling her side against the door, she took a deep breath, the motion of her chest causing the rings around her neck to sway and thump against her sternum. It wasn't the jewels that grabbed her mind's attention, but the slightly sharp crown of the Irish Claddagh ring. The tarnished and withered gold was the oldest remaining artifact of the Allaway line. She couldn't help but smirk. *And the four families think they have a twisted backstory. They've got nothing on the Allaways.*

"Come on, Buck," she almost giggled. "Let's go do some violence."

CHAPTER 12

One solid stomp on the edge of the bag sent the salt mixture under the door in a sudden whoosh. In the same moment, Basheba hurled herself against the door, surging out in the hall with Buck tucked close to her side. Mina slammed the door shut behind them, smothering the light from the hallway, and leaving them with only the glow seeping through the windows to see by. Basheba kept running as her eyes adjusted to the sudden darkness. Whatever had terrorized Mina and Ozzie had left its mark. A heavy stench filled the air, thick and gut-wrenching, a mixture of sulfur and rotten meat. It was a combination that hovered in the Witch Woods when *they* were around. It marked the presence of a demon.

Her heart thudded against her rib cage with renewed strength. She pushed herself harder, sprinting down the hallway until there was no way for her to slow down for the corner. She skidded across the threadbare carpet and slide-slammed the wall. Far more agile, Buck bounced off the wall, using it to surge forward and barrel down the stairs before her. The sound of his nails against the wooden floorboards faded into the depths of the house, and she was left alone in a smothering silence.

Basheba slowed to a cautious creep upon reaching the final few stairs. Adrenaline turned her pulse into deafening thunder in her ears, almost completely drowning out the soft creak of the stairs underfoot. Moonlight streamed through the front windows to pool over the scattered rugs. The yellowed glow of the cult's flaming torches flickered over the walls, casting strange shadows over the portraits, illuminating the white paint of their eyes more than anything else. While it left her feeling watched, she couldn't deny that the firelight soothed her. A familiar comfort in an alien environment.

Basheba kept to the walls, wading through the lagoon of dark shadows that remained gathered there. The unreliable light distorted the details of the rooms, but she recalled the simple layout well enough.

The silence unsettled her. It was thickened with the promise of the stories Isaac could have been feeding them. For whatever else he was, he was a Bell. He knew how she was trained to survive because he was trained in much the same way. Her mind's eye filled with an image of him stopping the men coming to kill her at the door, giving them some last-minute instructions. *Lure her out. Force her to come to you. Don't let her keep familiar ground.* Her fingers worked around the hilt of her knife. *You're not just a Bell,* she told herself. *You were trained to hunt, not just survive.*

Crouching low to keep from casting a shadow herself, she slipped under the window and reached for the lock on the front door. While she still hadn't settled on an actual plan, she knew she needed at least two bodies for it to work. Painful experience had taught her well enough that one dead body rarely served as sufficient warning. Still, she wasn't delusional enough to think she was in any position to fight the whole cult on her own.

The lock latched with a dull thud that resonated around the empty rooms. Her fingers roamed endlessly over the knife's hilt, adjusting and readjusting her grip while she strained to hear the slightest sound. Even Buck's movements were lost to her.

Crossing the room, she scanned it, keenly aware of any shift in the shadows. She almost jumped out of her skin when Cadwyn shattered the silence. The walls muffled his words, but the tone was clear enough. He was attempting to come to some kind of agreement with the cult. *Negotiator to the end*, she thought with a strange mixture of pity, jealousy, and amusement. A small part of her wondered what she could have been if she had been born a little bit more like him. *Dead, probably,* a voice whispered in the back of her head. *You'd be dead right now.*

Careful and cautious, she made her way through the house like a ghost. The conversation outside became a steady murmur, making it harder to pinpoint where the natural creaks and groans of the house were originating from. Random floorboards groaned in the distance. Coming and going too swiftly for her to lock eyes on the source. Restlessly, she tightened her grip on the knife, adrenaline making her palms prickle with sweat. Her heart hammered but she kept her breathing slow and steady.

She inched into the dining room. The glass doors allowed the moonlight to cut the room into a ladder of silver and shadows. Moving silently, she followed the length of the massive dining table, creeping from one dark patch to the next. A dark shadow lurched across the pools of moonlight, and she spun around to face the source. It wasn't the bullman. Someone of a similar build, but a far shorter stature. And vaguely familiar.

Her heart stammered with a fresh rush of adrenaline. *Hunting formation. One acts as a distraction while the other circles around.* It was a tactic she'd used more than once.

"Hey, you're one of the guys from the store," Basheba noted as she kept herself in motion, gaze flicking around, trying to track down the other man.

Clearly expecting a more terrified response, the man hesitated, seemingly not quite sure what to do next. He soon recovered and addressed her with a snarl.

"I'll give you a chance to make this easy. Although, I can't promise it'll be painless."

A dark mass crept out of the abyss, slowly pacing along the floor just behind the man. Silent and swift.

Basheba smiled, "Oh, this is going to hurt a lot."

Buck's growl broke the relative silence. His exposed fangs glistened in the minimal glow while his dark fur allowed him to blend into the gloom. The man turned, his eyes widening as the savage growl neared him. Buck's sharp snap shook him out of his daze.

"You're never—"

Basheba cut him off with a simple command. "Kill."

Buck lurched forward, combining his muscular strength and sheer weight to offset their would-be attacker. The man threw up an arm to fend him off, and the dog's jaws latched onto it. The sharp crack of bone echoed under the man's screams. The slick shredding of flesh joined with it. Buck didn't relent. Each time he was torn free, he simply found a new pound of flesh to sink his teeth into. The man's screams barely covered the jarring crack of his bones.

The grotesque noise covered the sounds of the man charging toward her until it was too late. Basheba turned just as the bull-man swung his massive fist. It caught her under her jaw and sent her flying back. Blood splashed across her tongue as she slammed into the wood floor.

"Call him off!" The bull-man bellowed.

Stars danced across Basheba's eyes and she realized she had hit the back of her head against the floor. Vaguely, she became aware of the knife still clutched in her hand.

"Call your mutt off!"

The bull-man leaped over the table with startling agility. He landed on top of her, his hands instantly going for her throat. The razor-sharp spikes of her collar sunk effortlessly into the tender flesh of his palms. Hot blood gushed over her neck as the man pulled back, howling with pain and fury. Basheba thrust herself up and, without hesitation, plunged the knife into the man's stomach, pushing in until the hilt pressed against his skin. He roared again, doubling over and throwing his fist down. Basheba slid herself back over the floor, narrowly missing the blow.

The screaming stopped as she got to her feet. Buck released his grip and the corpse dropped, motionless and silent.

Blood dripped from his snout as he turned to the bull-man. Shoulders hunched and head low, he prowled closer, snarling all the while. The bull-man pushed himself up onto his feet, trying to keep both Basheba and Buck in sight at the same time. At last, he glared at Basheba.

"You bitch."

She smiled, trying to hide how vulnerable she felt without her weapon in hand. Whatever injuries she had given him didn't seem to take away his strength. Buck's constant growl offered some reassurance. Enough to keep her spine straight and her head raised.

"Flattery isn't going to change things now," she said. "You could leave, get some medical attention."

With a feral smile curling his lips, the man slowly pulled the blade out. Blood bubbled free to stain the front of his shirt. In the dim light, it looked as black as tar and as polished as onyx.

"I'm going to murder you slowly," he promised.

"Now, that's just lazy."

Rage mangled his face as he charged toward her. Buck lunged at the same moment, landing on the man's back and latching onto his muscle-swelled shoulder. Basheba backed up a step. Everything within her skin went cold when the man lurched back. There was a heavy thud, a pained yelp, and Buck was tossed away. He slid across the dining table and off the other side, knocking over and breaking the chairs when he landed on them.

"Buck!"

She was so focused on her dog she almost missed the man's approach. Far smaller than him, she was able to dive under the table and roll out the other side. Buck was slumped amongst the wreckage of the chairs.

"Buck," she whispered.

With a savage grunt, the bull-man latched onto the end of the long table and hurled it to the side. The show of strength affected her more than she cared to admit. She longed to run. But the sight of Buck sprawled out made her turn on her heels and face her attacker.

"You hurt my dog!"

"I'm going to kill it right after I kill you." The bull-man grinned, brandishing the knife for her to see.

Rage ignited within her like a flashfire, scorching her fear and turning it to ash. She moved first, keeping low to force the man to bend is injured torso if he was to attempt another attack. He turned, trying to position himself, and swung the blade down. It sliced into her backpack, forcing her lower, knocking her off balance but giving her the opening she needed to rake her deadly wristband across the back of his ankle. The sharp spikes cut through his pant legs and into his flesh.

A pained cry left him and he buckled a bit, but the wound wasn't as deep as she had wanted. *Cut the Achille's heel. Bring them down.* The instructions she had been given so long ago had always served her well. She knew her size, her weakness, and how helpless she would be if she didn't get the upper hand somehow.

In a burst of motion, she gripped the side of the toppled table and leaped over it. The bull-man came for her swiftly. He slashed, bringing the blade a hair's breadth away from her face. Basheba struck out at his retreating hand, slicing his wrist open. He bellowed and hunched over the table, trying to reach her, spraying blood from his wound in his fury. A pained gasp for air left the man's lungs as Buck bounded onto his back. The dog latched his jaws around the back of the bull-man's neck.

Basheba burst forward. With the weight on his back, the wound in his gut, and the jaws locked onto his neck, there was no way for him to escape the coming blow. Basheba swung with all the strength her small body was capable of, driving her arm up and embedding the spikes of her wristband into the man's eye.

A wave of hot blood washed out over her skin as the man trembled and screamed, then dropped her knife. It came and went in a moment. The growing puddle of blood caught her feet and she slipped and tumbled to the ground. Buck was beside her in an instant, nuzzling her with concern and licking the sweat from her brow.

"Are you okay?" she asked, patting whatever patches of fur she could reach under his armor, offering reassurance while looking for any injuries.

He was just stunned. She almost wept with relief.

"You had me worried, you drama queen," she whispered into his fur as she hugged his neck.

A raspy, gargled sound pierced the stillness. She lurched back from Buck, grabbing the discarded knife and ready to strike. The bull-man remained slumped in the crumpled heap Buck had left him in. The stark white of his bone jutted through the tendons and flesh of his neck as blood pooled beneath him. He dragged in another breath, releasing the ghastly sound once more. Muscles twitched and strained in his jaw, but he couldn't work his head off the ground.

"I can't move," he rasped.

Basheba slowly got to her feet, eyeing the spinal cord that glistened with ebony blood in the hazy glow. Fire crackled outside and the cult restlessly stirred, but no one came to help. *They assume these guys can kill a little girl on their own.*

Basheba sucked in a breath through her teeth and winced. "Yeah, your neck is broken. I don't think you're getting back up." She scanned the room to reassure herself that no one else was lurking about. The corpse of his companion and the liquor cabinet helping to forge a plan in the back of her head.

"This is awkward," she cut in over the man's snarled threats and curses. "But I kind of need you dead. You only have yourself to blame, so I don't want you getting bitter about the whole situation."

His remaining eye rolled up to glare at her as she approached.

"You don't have it in you."

"Oh," she hissed. "Now it's more awkward. You're not my first. Sorry."

The knowledge settled on the man and he began to thrash as best his broken body could. It was little more than a shark toss of his head.

"You'll die for this!"

"Don't be bitter," she dismissed, crouching down next to him.

"They'll come for you."

"They're not even coming for you," she countered. "I think I have pretty good odds against a bunch of cowards. They'll probably take care of themselves once they see you're dead."

The man's blood-stained teeth flashed as he chuckled, deep and cold. "You little idiot. There are others to take my place."

"I did view you as expendable."

"You best hope she doesn't take control," he said, grinning to himself. "You think I'm bad?"

"Not particularly," Basheba said, only to be ignored.

The man was determined that his last words would carry the threat.

"The one who takes my place is so much worse than me. Blood-thirsty and savage. She'll destroy you all. She'll rip your soul to shreds."

His laughter grew, echoing off the walls even as his lungs began to fill with blood. Basheba patted the back of his head gently with one hand before driving the hunting knife deep into his remaining eye. His laughter cut off into a violent trembling, his nervous system spasming with the last throes of his dying brain. It only lasted a moment and then they were left in silence. Jerking her blade free, she rocked back on her heels and glanced at Buck. His nails scraped over the floorboard as he squirmed with barely contained energy.

"We're going to need rope and that broken chair." A new thought struck her and she bit back a smile. It was long past time for Uncle Isaac to learn just what he was messing with. "It's a special occasion, Buck. Let's go for some shock and awe. Go fetch the whiskey."

CHAPTER 13

Cadwyn lingered by the window, watching the cult members squirm restlessly. Their anxious energy bled into the room, making Mina pace back and forth while Ozzie sat on the bed, completely at a loss for what to do with his hands.

"It's taking too long," Mina said, twisting around on her toes to retrace her path. "Everything went silent fifteen minutes ago. Something has obviously happened to her."

"Just breathe," Cadwyn said absently. He was too busy trying to keep Isaac in sight, to pay much attention to her anxieties.

Every so often, the older man would feel the weight of Cadwyn's attention and tip his face up to glare at him.

If the situation were different, Cadwyn would have laughed. Compared to the sheer murderous fury Basheba effortlessly wielded in her eyes, the man's scowl had the air of a toddler's temper tantrum.

"Do you think she's okay?" Ozzie asked.

"I have every faith that she is," Cadwyn reassured.

In the corner of his eyes, he watched Ozzie look up at him, his fingers wringing in the comforter.

"How can you be so sure?"

"Because it's Basheba," Cadwyn said with a wry smile. "You only ever have to worry about the people in her way."

"What did she mean?" Mina mumbled.

"Are you talking to us or yourself?" Ozzie asked.

The question startled Mina. She paused, looking at them both in turn before elaborating on the thought that had slipped from her mouth.

"I was just thinking about the message Basheba passed on to Isaac. 'Come near me again, and I'll show you exactly what I did to the others,'" she quoted. "What did she mean by that? What did she do?"

Cadwyn frowned, rapidly reaching the limits of his tolerance for the girls' feud. "Are you sure that's what you should be focusing on at the moment?"

Mina shrugged as she wrapped her arms protectively around her torso. "We've been here for fifteen minutes. I've already obsessed over my father, my ignorance of my family dynamics, the demon, the flaws of my plan, and the cult outside. This was just the next thing on the list."

Ozzie's heavy brow inched up his forehead. "You've already worried about all that?"

"Of course. Haven't you?"

"I'm still stuck on the cult," he said, awkwardly gesturing to the window.

She turned to Cadwyn for backup.

"I've been rather busy keeping watch," he said.

Mina deflated somewhat and returned to her self-soothing habit of pacing. "Jeremiah always tells me I worry too much."

"That's your brother, right?" Ozzie asked.

Mina nodded rapidly, her gaze already clouding over with unspoken thoughts.

When the room fell once more into unbearable silence, Ozzie tried again to break the tension.

"How's he doing?"

"Good," she mumbled absently. "He's dating someone, but hasn't mentioned it to the family, yet." Pausing again, her head perked up. "Why are they hesitating? They could just storm the place."

Cadwyn looked out the window again, once more making eye contact with the incensed Isaac.

"Because they know there's a demon in here."

"Well, that's a good sign, right?" Ozzie said, hands fluttering as if he could somehow grasp a silver lining. "I mean, it backs up Basheba's theory that they won't follow us into the woods."

"Great," Mina mumbled, pacing again. "The wolves won't follow us into shark-infested waters."

"You sound like your dad," Cadwyn mentioned absently.

He could feel Mina staring a hole in his back.

"How much do you know about my father?"

"Enough to lean more toward Percival's perspective of him than yours."

Ozzie's fingers drummed against his knees, latching onto the passing hope for a change in conversation. "You're friends with my godfather? Um, father. Wow, that's still really weird to say."

"I wouldn't say we're friends," Cadwyn said. When Ozzie's shoulders slumped, he quickly added, "He's a man I greatly respect, we just don't run in the same circles."

For the briefest moment, Ozzie seemed content, proud to know that his lifelong friend was held in high regard. It struck Cadwyn anew just how much had been thrust upon the boy. Cadwyn didn't have any first-hand knowledge about Percival Sewall's relationship with the Davis couple. Rumor had it, he had dated Ha-Yun before they all came to the mutual conclusion that she was better suited for Percival's best friend, Ethan.

The whirlwind romance that followed had seen the new couple married, with Percival as their best man, before they even knew Ha-Yun was pregnant. Somehow, they had all stayed good friends despite what had to be an awkward situation. Seemingly the only sticking point of the dynamic was that the Davis family refused to tell Ozzie who his father was, and all the connotations of having the blood of a Sewall. But the Bell Witch had known. She had given him her music box and selected him for her Harvest the previous autumn. In the space of three days, Ozzie's entire world had crumbled down around him, burying him in the smoldering wreckage. Cadwyn still found himself in awe that the teenager had managed to crawl his way out.

"What did she do?" Mina mumbled to herself, breaking Cadwyn

free of his thoughts.

"I don't think it matters right now," Ozzie said as tactfully as he could.

Mina continued her pacing, one arm still wrapped around her torso while her other hand tapped the ends of her hair against her bottom lip. Cadwyn had never known that such a move could look thoughtful.

"It is, so long as Isaac's leading the charge," Mina said. "Did you notice how they only said they wanted Basheba?"

"They were obviously lying," Cadwyn said.

"Perhaps they were, but I don't think Isaac was," Mina said.

Ozzie's hands rubbed his legs again, a helpless search for reassurance.

"What do you mean?" he asked.

"I don't know what the message was about, but it was clearly a threat. And suddenly, here he is with a mob for backup. I think, for him at least, this whole thing isn't about appeasing the Witch. I think he's trying to eliminate Basheba before she can follow through on her promise."

Cadwyn was the first to dismiss it, saying, "None of that matters."

"I don't want to get drawn into a family feud unaware."

"Why not? We've all been into your family business," Cadwyn said.

She bristled. "What do you mean by that?"

Sucking in a deep breath, he closed his eyes, kicking himself for opening that particular Pandora's box. A series of shouts caught them all off guard. Ozzie and Mina rushed to the window, crowding in front of him to press against the glass. He was easily able to look over their heads but wasn't all that excited with them being in clear view of the people below.

Cadwyn's muscles tensed when the first person pointed toward them. In the space of a heartbeat, he realized they weren't looking at them, but at the rooftop. Like a rising tide, more in the mob lifted their heads to focus above them. It churned his stomach to wonder what they were looking at. Cautiously, Mina pushed the window open a crack. The scent of smoke and apple blossoms flooded the room. Murmured voices became sharp and clear. The combination left Cadwyn inescapably aware that there was no real separation between them. No safe place to hide.

As the first spike of fear subsided, his brow furrowed. "Where's their leader?"

Mina and Ozzie both threw him a questioning look before reexamining the crowd. Frustrated murmurs rippled through the group, growing in fever as the people twisted and turned, searching the crowd just as much as their three prisoners did. The bull-man didn't return. Cadwyn's mouth quirked into a smirk.

"She got him," he whispered.

A sharp bar of tension loosened, allowing him to take a deep breath.

"You seem proud of her," Mina said.

"Aren't you?" Cadwyn asked. "The woman has talents."

She tipped her head, trying for a shrug, but too tense to pull it off.

"I guess my perspective is off," Mina said, "having been on the receiving end of her talents."

"You didn't die. Don't exaggerate," Cadwyn said with a growing smile.

The lift of Mina's chin resembled the princess she was at heart. "You sound like Basheba."

His grin was lost when the girl didn't turn to see it. What little amount of levity he had managed to cultivate was shattered when Isaac stormed to the front.

"Basheba!" Isaac snarled. "Why must you make everything difficult?"

"Boredom, mostly."

Cadwyn released a long breath to hear his friend's voice. He had never considered that she wouldn't be able to handle herself, but it felt good to know she was unscathed enough to maintain her sass.

Isaac stewed in his inept rage before Whitney made her way from the crowd. Basheba's past observation lingered in Cadwyn's mind. It startled him slightly to know he wasn't the only one contemplating the theory.

"If she's right," Mina mumbled to herself, "and an excess of fat or muscle is proof of the Witch's favor, then Whitney's one of her favorites."

"She's not that heavy," Ozzie defended.

Cadwyn and Mina both looked at him with raised eyebrows.

"She's 300 pounds, minimum," Cadwyn said. "That's morbidly obese."

Ozzie cringed. "Yeah, maybe, but you're not supposed to talk about stuff like that."

"I'm a nurse," Cadwyn reminded. "Noticing and remarking on possible health problems is literally part of my job."

"Yeah, okay, but..." Ozzie lowered his voice to a strained whisper, as if the woman below might overhear them. "It still feels mean to say it, though."

"She's actively trying to murder us," Mina noted. "I don't give a damn about her feelings."

Once the mob noticed Whitney's movements, they parted for her, allowing her to strut to Isaac's side. The firelight from the nearest torch cast her face in dancing shadows but couldn't diminish the vibrancy of her lipstick. Her mouth was pulled as taut as the skin around her eyes as she glared up at the rooftop.

"Where is Timothy?" Whitney demanded.

"Who the hell is Timmy?" Basheba shot back. "Nah, I'm just kidding. I don't care."

"Everything is a joke to you, isn't it?" Whitney snarled.

"You most certainly are," Basheba said.

Cadwyn chuckled, the sound bristling over his nerves, and whispered, "She walked into that one."

Isaac didn't share Cadwyn's amusement. Growling out a sigh, the older man shoved his wire-rimmed glasses higher up on his nose.

"I suppose it was too much to expect you to face the consequences of your actions with any amount of dignity."

"Have I disappointed you, Uncle? Oh, please, come in so we can discuss this face to face."

Cadwyn didn't need to see her to know the feral smile that accompanied her words. Still, he leaned forward slightly, cautiously, trying to catch a glimpse of her. Isaac bristled, squaring his shoulders and clenching his jaw. All his posturing to look strong only highlighted his desperation.

"He's always seemed like a jumpy guy to me," Ozzie whispered.

"This is different somehow," Cadwyn said, eyeing the man carefully.

Mina made a sound similar to a bitter snort. "His crown's slipping. Father said he made 'arrangements.' I'm guessing he asked for quite a lot in exchange for handing over Basheba."

"It's remarkable how little that man learns from his mistakes," Cadwyn said.

"But, what did he ask for in return?" Ozzie squeaked.

A flood of horrible options flooded Cadwyn's mind but there wasn't time to contemplate any of it.

Isaac collected himself and stormed a few feet closer to the house, still cautious to keep out of striking range. *At least he's smart enough to know she won't be unarmed,* Cadwyn thought.

"I think it's clear we don't see eye to eye!"

"I despise you with every fiber of my being," Basheba cut in casually. "But go on."

"But you are family! The Bell blood flows through your veins as much as mine! For the love of your father, of all those we have lost, I beseech you to listen to reason!"

"Let them kill me?"

"It has to come to an end," Isaac bellowed. "You have to have known this day would come! You can't deny your nature forever! You're a Bell woman, Basheba! If you had merely acted in accordance with the demands of your ancestors, all of this could have been avoided! Don't make it worse. For the memory of your father, my beloved brother, do what you were born to do!"

Heavy silence followed, broken only by the crackle of the open flames.

"That's some blatant emotional manipulation," Mina muttered.

Ozzie's mouth scrunched up in disgust. "What a scumbag."

"Go get your things," Cadwyn said with as much calm as he could muster. They hesitated, and he nudged their shoulders. "Now."

Too late. Basheba's voice, cold as an arctic breeze while still sweetly pleasant, drew everyone's attention.

"You're right, Uncle."

A smirk pulled at Isaac's lips.

"I should follow the example of my ancestors. But I'm not just a Bell."

Cadwyn jerked at the first high-pitched scream. An instant later, a colossal shadow streaked across the window. The noose wrapped around the man's neck brought the body to a sudden jolt. He only realized Basheba had split open the man's stomach when the jolt spilled the man's innards. The screams grew louder as the body swung back. Cadwyn barely had time to twist around and shelter the smaller two before the body crashed through the window. Shards of glass pattered against Cadwyn's biker jacket.

Shock rattled them all when they turned back to see the leader of the cult twisting on a noose, his intestines dropping from the wide hole in his stomach, a severed hunk of kidney slowly trickling down his legs. The next round of screams came a split second before the next body crashed through the other window, disemboweled and limp. The mob below worked into a fevered panic. Horrified and rattled to see the brutality they had wanted to inflict instead turned onto two of their own.

"I will eat your heart!" Basheba bellowed, her voice distorted with feral delights and bloodlust.

The wind changed, bringing with it the stench of whiskey. Cadwyn shoved the others away from the window just as fire sizzled down the length of the rope and reached the man's liquor drenched clothes. The fire wouldn't last long, he knew. But the initial flash was scorching and the first lapping flames impressive. The panicked screams turned to sorrowful wails, blood-chilling and shrill. Golden light filled the room, bringing with it the overpowering stench of burning flesh. Cadwyn answered the phone vibrating in his pocket without ever taking his wide eyes off the ghastly sight.

"That was the distraction, idiots," Basheba's voice was as calm and pleasant as it could ever be. "Do me a favor? I'm going to lure them around back. Can you get my hunting bow out of my car? It's in a compartment under the mattress."

"Hunting bow?" he asked numbly.

Shaking himself out of his shock, he turned and began manhandling the others, forcing them to get their stuff and head to the door.

"Yeah, I prefer my knife, but I think we're going to need it."

"I'll get it," he mumbled, barely aware that his mouth was moving.

"This is why I'm willing to marry you," she teased.

"Well, this and my great health care plan."

"Obviously," she laughed. "See you in the Witch Woods."

And with that, she hung up.

Chapter 14

Mina choked on her scream as the flaming bodies consumed her vision. Already, the flames were starting to dwindle as the alcohol burned up, but they still lashed violently, hot enough that it burned her eyes to see it. Ozzie grabbed her shoulder, yanking her out of her horrified stupor. She staggered along with his persistent pulling, only turning after she had been shoved out into the hall.

"Bathroom," Cadwyn commanded, closing the door behind them and locking it in place before sliding the key under the door.

Ozzie twisted his hand in the collar of her shirt, refusing to let go even as they ran together. Solid thuds echoed from the darkness downstairs. The house shook as the cult threw themselves against the front door, trying and failing to break it down. Cadwyn appeared at their backs, shoving them into the bathroom, barely able to close the door before the sound of shattering glass allowed the enraged voices inside.

Cadwyn swiftly locked the bathroom door and tied the shower curtain around the handle. Watching him, her thoughts began to emerge from the panicked haze of her mind.

"My bag," Mina mumbled.

"I've got it," Ozzie said in a whisper.

With numb fingers, she took her backpack from him, feeling the depth of her ineptitude like bitter bile on her tongue. Moonlight spilled through the high set window, turning Cadwyn into a looming shadow. He straightened from his task, his long arms stretching out to herd them like lost ducklings.

"Window," he whispered, his voice almost lost under the rampage below.

He was the only one tall enough to reach it. After pushing it open, Cadwyn braced his back against the wall and cupped his hands, giving Ozzie the boost he needed to squeeze through the gap. He awkwardly fumbled before dropping out of sight. Mina's breath caught. It was a physical effort to keep her panicked cry silent, not wanting to draw the attention of the mob that was storming toward them.

"There's a landing," Cadwyn said, his hand roughly cupping the back of her head and yanking her closer.

They scrambled against each other, her awkward movements accidentally striking the wound on his thigh before she managed to find the cup of his hands. He jerked her up. She swung her bag out first and braced herself against the windowsill. Despite her best efforts, she still had to step on Cadwyn's shoulder to get the last of the way out.

The short drop onto the roof tiles didn't give her enough time to brace herself. Pain sliced through her bones as she smacked against the unrelenting surface. She slid a few inches down the slight slope before she managed to find purchase.

"Are you okay?" Ozzie asked.

She nodded once, clenching her teeth against the lingering pain. He skittered into the shadows. It took her half a second to realize that Cadwyn didn't have any helping hand. Pushing herself up, she twisted around only to find Ozzie retreating from the window. The sounds of the bathroom door being ripped apart followed Cadwyn out as he slipped from the gap with more grace than either of them had managed to summon. In a nearly impossible maneuver, he rolled across his shoulders, bringing the long expanse of his body to a stop by planting one foot against the roof tiles.

"How?" Ozzie whispered.

Cadwyn's bangs dropped into his eyes in a sweaty tangle. The moonlight made the fresh blood seeping through his pants look like oil.

"I've added parkour into my workout routine," Cadwyn spoke in a whisper as he ushered them up to the side of the building, forcing them into the shadows and out of the sight of the people still breaking down the bathroom door. "After our experience in the woods, I figured it would be a useful skill."

Mina knew he was only speaking in an attempt to keep them calm. A part of her resented being handled with kid gloves. A small, bitter part that detested her own weakness. Still, she couldn't help but cling to the small offer of normalcy.

Cadwyn kept them wedged between the wall and his own body, his black biker jacket allowing him to shield them like a shadow as they moved to the corner. Firelight from the burning men danced before her, far dimmer now than it had been before. The smell remained, though. Thick and heavy and nauseating. She tried not to think about what they were moving toward. Or the fact that they were effectively heading right back to the room they had fled. With terror twisting her gut and clouding her thoughts, she knew she wasn't in any condition to suggest an alternative plan. Instead, she focused on mimicking Cadwyn's light tread. It startled her to realize just how graceless she was.

When they reached the front corner of the building, Cadwyn pressed a hand against Mina's stomach to bring her to a stop. Straining his towering form in a way that must have been agony for his legs, he glanced around the corner.

"Go," he whispered. "Don't look."

The rhythmic thud against the door suddenly changed, signaling the cult had finally broken through. Cadwyn grabbed Ozzie by the back of his neck and hurled him around the corner first, following a step behind. All three of them pressed their spines against the wood, freezing in place and fighting their panting breaths to keep silent. Mina's full focus locked on the noises echoing from the bathroom. *They have to know we're out here,* she thought. Images filled her mind. Images of the cult dividing and spilling out onto the ledge to follow them. Half coming from the bathroom while the others clawed free of the shattered bedroom windows. *We're trapped.*

The rope released a low creak before it snapped. The smoldering corpse dropped like a stone, landing on the porch steps with a nauseating squelch. Mina squeezed her eyes closed and tried not to look, but her mind supplied a vivid image anyway. Every second pressed down upon her like heavy stones, crushing her lungs and thickening the air until she choked on each breath. The touch of the evening breeze reminded her just how exposed she was. Flickering firelight played across her eyelids like a spotlight. She flinched when she heard what she had dreaded. Harsh voices and heavy footsteps coming from both sides. Mina clenched her jaw and lifted her chin, trying to prepare herself for what was coming.

A bloodcurdling scream sliced through the night, making her jump so hard she almost lost her footing. As the sound ebbed away, Mina held her breath again, sure that even her heartbeat would reveal their position in the resulting silence. All at once, footsteps stampeded away, flowing back into the depths of the house and out of earshot. She slumped as she released her breath.

"Why didn't they come out?" Ozzie asked.

Cadwyn grinned, a brilliant flash of straight white teeth. "They're too big."

The relief in his voice was proof that all of it had been a gamble. Cadwyn refused to let them move until the night stilled, leaving only the crackling, sputtering fire to disturb the silence. Carefully, he skidded to the edge of the roof ledge. He crouched low to check that the coast was clear. While the drugs in his system took the edge off the pain, a fresh wave of blood seeped out. Enough that Mina worried he had pulled a stitch. He waved them over.

"When I lower you down, I want you to hide in the crawlspace," he whispered. "Wait there until I come for you. I have to do something for Basheba."

"Crawlspace?" Ozzie asked, clearly baffled.

Mina squeezed his hand, reassuring him that he just had to follow her. *I can lead the way. I can do this. Don't freeze.* Cadwyn sat down and dug his heels into the groove of the drainage pipe. Mina went first.

They linked arms and, with his elbows locked against his sides, he slowly lowered her down. It was an impressive amount of strength, and she only jolted slightly, her feet blindly groping for porch fencing. She found it and scrambled down to keep watch while Ozzie was lowered next. His foot slipped on the railing and he fell backward into the flower bushes that lined the building. Mina had to crawl over the porch railing since the burning corpse was still on the stairs. She found him writhing in the foliage. Approaching sounds of footsteps made her heart jerk and she released the railing, dropping down out of sight.

Mina and Ozzie shared a wide-eyed stare as they waited. A heavy click and the door slowly opened. She shoved Ozzie's shoulder, using her other hand to point out the small gap under the stairs, the passage illuminated by the smoldering remains. The gap was just big enough for them to slither through.

Rich-smelling earth shifted under them as they clawed their way into the minimal hiding space. She hoped the relative darkness would be enough to keep the signs of disturbance from being too obvious. They were still situating themselves when the floorboards creaked. A shadow draped over them, cold and deep, while the fire's warmth pressed against her face. Ozzie's fingers found hers. Without a word, they clutched at each other, each tightening their grip until it hurt. The footsteps paused just above their heads.

Mina could feel her heartbeat in her throat. It was impossible to tell which one of them was trembling, but her arm shook with it all the same. Unable to take the tension squirming in her gut like live snakes, Mina glanced up, peeking between the floorboards. A scream ripped from her throat as the head of an ax drove down. Wood splintered in the wake of the deadly blade. Mina flattened herself against the earth, staring in horror at the deadly tip that would have cleaved her head in two if the thicker butt of the ax head hadn't become wedged in place.

With a sharp jerk, the ax was wrenched free, raining splinters down upon her face. Mina couldn't help but stare up at the man through the gap. Long, matted tendrils of hair framed his face, taking on the same hue of the firelight. The shadows did nothing to diminish the pure disgust that radiated from his pale eyes. She hadn't thought it would be possible for a complete stranger to hate her that much. It took her breath away like a vice squeezing her lungs. It was only when he reared the ax back for another blow that she was broken out of her shock. She slid over the loose earth and twisted around, scrambling on hands and knees to go deeper into the shadows.

The man's beefy hand slipped through the gap with the speed of a snake strike. Pain sizzled up the length of her leg as the man's tightening grip crushed her ankle. She kicked back with her free foot, blindly crunching her heel against the man's fingers. His hand retreated to be replaced with another strike of the ax, the blade narrowly missing her foot as she burst forward. Ozzie waited for her a few feet ahead, barely visible in the lingering shadows.

"Are you all right?" he asked, voice higher than normal and eyes wide.

"Yeah. Go. Just go."

The wood continued to crack apart behind them, but it didn't take too long for their attacker to realize he wouldn't be able to follow. Footsteps thundered above them, closing in, pausing above them once more. Ozzie and Mina rolled to different sides as the ax blade broke through the floorboard. This time gouging deeper, almost hitting the earth. Coming to a stop, Mina looked to Ozzie. A desperate attempt to form some kind of plan with him to keep them from being separated. Somehow, Ozzie interpreted the glance to be some kind of direction. He nodded and skittered forward. Mina burst into motion to follow. The ax blows continued to chop through the floorboards. Sometimes, it was close enough to nip at their flesh, while, at other times, the blows landed far from them, offering them slithers of hope that the man had lost track of them.

"What are you doing!"

The sudden outburst made Mina flatten herself against the soil. A few feet away, Ozzie did the same. Panting hard, they shared a panicked glance before both tried to see through the flooring. It took her a moment to realize she recognized the voice.

'Whitney,' she mouthed to Ozzie.

His heavy brow furrowed before he returned his attention to the conversation happening above.

"They're in the crawlspace," the muscled mand huffed.

"So you destroy my place? Get out of the way!"

In a burst of movement, Ozzie scurried across the area of damage and rejoined Mina's side. Firelight washed through the ax holes. Together, Mina and Ozzie cringed away from the largest gap, trying to keep the growing light from touching them. A hard thud resounded just before Whitney's face filled the gap. A sweet smile stretched her face as she purred down to them.

"Hello, little darlings. Did Eddy scare you? He can be such a brute. Come on, now. Come out."

Ozzie leaned heavily against Mina's side, trying to get further away from the woman.

"Is she serious?" he whispered.

"We won't hurt you," Whitney continued in her sickly-sweet tone.

Her face shifted across the gap, trying to get a decent look at them.

"We only want Basheba," she continued. "Leave her behind and you're free to go."

"Why her?" Mina asked, half regretting making any conversation at all. But she had to know; needed to peel back the layers of lies and deceit that shrouded her life, and find the truth in something.

"You needn't concern yourself with that. Come on, now. I'll get you both some tea. I made a Bee Sting cake today. It's delicious."

Mina and Ozzie shared a bewildered look.

"Why do I feel like she's trying to plump us up to eat us?" he whispered.

Clearing her throat, Mina spoke with all the confidence she didn't feel. "I'm not going anywhere until you answer my question."

"You're in no position to make demands, little princess," Whitney said.

"Is it because of Isaac?" Mina pushed. "What did he promise you? The man's a notorious liar."

"You'll never understand, little princess. Let's get you back to your daddy. The Witch will take you when she wishes it."

"Whitney!" It was a voice that Mina didn't recognize, but the panic within it alarmed her.

She flinched again when something struck her on the back. Turning around, she hurriedly scanned the darkness, finding Cadwyn crouched by a small gap. He waved them over. Tapping Ozzie's shoulder, she sent him first, still straining to hear the conversation happening above.

"She's making her way to the bullpen," the stranger said.

"Good," Whitney said. "He'll take care of her."

"But," the man stammered.

"But what?" Whitney snapped. "She's one scared little girl. Kill the dog and she'll be nothing."

"She's already killed three of us," the stranger protested.

"The dog did."

"The dog didn't gut them."

Whitney's voice took on an icy edge. "Watch your tone."

"Of course," the stranger whispered. "I'm just saying, I don't think Isaac told us the truth about her. It makes me nervous as to why he's so insistent."

"The Witch wants her."

"So he says," the stranger added nervously.

Whitney was silent for a moment before she hissed out. "Kill her. And someone bring Isaac to me!"

Another clump of earth hit her. An impatient reminder that she had to move. She continued to strain for every word as she retreated to the opening. Cadwyn dragged her out the rest of the way the second she came into reach. Even the shadows couldn't hide his anger.

"The cult didn't pick Basheba as their sacrifice. Isaac did," she said in a rushed whisper.

Cadwyn's brow furrowed, the implication striking him like a physical blow. *Dad was wrong,* Mina thought. *Isaac isn't just following the cult in a desperate bid to survive. He has sway over them.* Shaking off the shock, Cadwyn lifted his head and jerked to the shadows of the driveway.

"I thought we were meeting Basheba in the woods," Ozzie said.

"We are," Cadwyn assured in a whisper. "But she's lured them that way. I can't get you both past them unseen. There're fewer people minding the road."

Once more, the older man positioned himself to be their shield. Mina absently noted the contraption in his hand. It looked too small for him. A mangled archery bow, the tips bending in at an odd angle and tipped with wheels. A cylinder was strapped across his back. It too looked like a child's toy as it rested against his broad shoulders.

The crunch of the gravel under their feet sounded like screams in the darkness. Voices murmured from the distance. Shouts and demands met with the low bellow of a bull. Adrenaline made her stomach roll and her hands shake. Her shoulder brushed Ozzie's as they clustered close to each other, both finely tuned to any change in Cadwyn's posture. More than once, he ushered them into the darkness under the tree limbs. The scent of apple blossoms hit her nose. A pleasant sweetness that engulfed them as they huddled in the shadows, waiting for the people to pass.

After the third time, Cadwyn kept them just behind the tree line, regardless of how it clearly agitated him. Despite the distance they put between them, the screams only grew louder. One shriek broke above it all. Agonized and feral and unmistakably female. Cadwyn whipped around at the noise, his jaw hanging low and his eyes wide. He forced them all to break into a run.

Chapter 15

Ozzie had thought it would be easier to keep up with Cadwyn in the woods, where the tangled mass of branches would work against the man's height. But Cadwyn's sure stride never faltered. His movements were clear and precise as he threaded his towering form through gaps in the foliage that Ozzie didn't even know were there. Every few yards, Cadwyn had to slow down and wait for them to catch up. Guilt trickled through his fear to pool in the pit of his gut.

I'm going to get better, Ozzie resolved. He clung to that determination to silence the little voice that questioned if he'd ever have the chance.

At last, they approached a clearing, noticeable only by the way it glowed. Leaves and flowers diffused the moonlight, painting the air with a silver haze. Cadwyn slowed at last, chest heaving and eyes darting. Ozzie found a moss-covered log and crouched low behind it with Mina. Both of them waited anxiously to catch Cadwyn's eyes and waved him over.

"How's your leg?" Mina asked when the older man crouched down beside her.

"I'll fix it up after this," he whispered absently. "Can you see her?"

Ozzie poked his head up just enough to see over the log. The brilliance of the meadow all but killed his night vision. "Where's the paddock?"

Before Cadwyn could point it out, the stillness around them was broken by the sharp rustle of snapping branches. Torchlight flickered through the clustered leaves. All at once, Basheba burst into the meadow, announced by an explosion of petals. A hulking woman stormed after her. Her outstretched hand clawed at Basheba's spine, unable to get a grip as the smaller girl suddenly leaped like a startled fawn and dropped to the ground. Ozzie lurched up to help but Cadwyn was quicker, grabbing his wrist and dragging him back down into the hiding place. Pain sparked through his knees as they collided with the earth again. The pain was forgotten when he heard a strange 'twang.'

A branch snapped around, swinging over Basheba's body to smack hard against the woman's chest. She took the impact and just stood there, branch flush against her breasts, her mouth gaping like a fish.

"Ozzie, look away," Cadwyn whispered.

He didn't understand why until he noticed the black stain working its way across the front of the stranger's shirt. *Blood.* Even the thought made his stomach roil. His heartbeat picked up, leaving his head spinning and his skin damp with cold sweat. Basheba jumped to her feet and started struggling with the branch. In the end, she had to wedge her foot against the woman's stomach and throw her weight into it. Basheba's hunting knife slipped from the stranger's flesh, dark and dripping with blood. That done, Basheba left the woman to slump lifelessly to the earth, more occupied with fussing in the shadows.

"She knows how to set up booby traps?" Mina muttered.

Cadwyn swallowed thickly but tried not to look disturbed. "Aren't you glad you're on her good side?"

Basheba whistled and Buck lunged from the darkness. After receiving a few pats, the ever-obedient dog took the order to drag the body back to his hiding place. Ozzie scrambled up again when he noticed Basheba turn away.

"Hey," he whispered harshly, not quite sure how many people he might attract.

It was still enough to make Basheba whip around. Ozzie's heart staggered, certain she was about to hit the tripwire. It didn't happen.

"Hey, you guys made it," she beamed, the mud streaking her face making her teeth seem all the brighter. Tipping her head to the side, she shook a few leaves loose from her hair. "I'm actually pretty happy you're all alive."

"Is that a booby trap?" Mina asked numbly.

Basheba looked behind her as if she had only just noticed it. "So it is. Huh. Strange." She shrugged. "Should we go? I'll get my knife."

"How did you learn to do that?" Ozzie asked.

"How many have you killed?" Mina said at the same time. She caught the strange looks and furrowed her brow. "That wasn't an escape tactic. She was *luring* people in."

"We can discuss this after we flee for our lives," Cadwyn said coldly.

Mina's shoulders hunched like a chastised child. Basheba bled into the darkness, returning an instant later with hurried backward steps. The trees rustled as a man emerged in hot pursuit. One thick hand grabbed her wrist while the other brought a handgun within an inch of her nose.

"Uh, uh, uh, little girl," he grumbled. "No more running. No more tricks."

Basheba quirked an eyebrow, seemingly completely unaware of the gun. "Don't suppose you feel like taking a step to your right?"

Cadwyn surged forward a step, hesitating when the gun was turned onto him, but only stopping completely when another man emerged from behind Mina, his rifle already high and at the ready. The men grinned wildly at each other, a few gleeful chuckles slipping their lips.

"You city folks should have known better than to take this fight into the woods," the man holding the rifle sneered. "You're not hunters."

"*They're* not," Basheba corrected, sounding as if she was discussing the weather.

The man squeezed Basheba's arm, jerking her close as if he wanted to rip her shoulder from its socket. The small blonde winced but refused to release any sound of pain. Cadwyn jerked, then kept still as the second man trained his rifle on him. Ozzie's hands started to shake uncontrollably.

"Oh, you're a big bad hunter, are you?" The man holding the tiny blonde grinned.

She tilted up her chin. "My whole family line was."

The man scoffed, moving the gun just far enough away that his face could take its place.

"Bells are nothing more than little rabbits running from the fox."

Basheba lowered her voice, drawing the man closer still.

"I'm not just a Bell. And ghosts aren't what I was trained to hunt."

The two men chuckled, sharing wide grins.

"And what do you hunt?" the man holding the rifle asked.

Basheba met their smile with one of her own. Gentle, shy, and every bit a Disney princess, she replied, "Long pig."

The movement was a blur. A dozen things happened at once, all overlapping and melding in Ozzie's head. Basheba lunged toward the man holding her. She stomped her right foot against his thigh to boost herself up while she drew her left knee to her chest, her shin pushing against the man's forearm. He fired blindly as his arm was forced wide. The single shot boomed like thunder.

Cadwyn spun around, ready to throw himself on the other attacker. A black mass bled from the abyss, silent and swift. *Buck.* The man fought against the enormous Rottweiler. But, with Buck's body keeping his rifle uselessly by his side, he didn't stand much of a chance. Ozzie turned, intent on helping Basheba, only to find she had locked her limbs around the man that had once held her.

The tiny woman dug her teeth deep into his throat. He bellowed. Another bite, along with a sharp shake of her head, and the sound was replaced by a gurgling rasp.

Blood gushed from his neck like a river of liquid onyx, frothing and spluttering from his mouth. It poured to the ground like grotesque rain. A spasm of shocked pain sent the gun toppling from the man's hand. He clawed and pounded at Basheba. With a wild growl, he wrenched her free and tossed her to the ground. Basheba bounced across the ground, kicking up the leaves and flower petals in her wake. Then she caught herself, arranging her limbs into a deep crouch, and time made sense again to Ozzie, ticking by at a normal pace.

Foliage swirled through the silver air, engulfing Basheba in a halo of shifting shadows. She drew herself up to her full height, the movement swift despite the blow she had taken. Blood poured from her lips, covered her jaw, and drenched her shirt. Steadily, she began to stalk, her steps silent but sure. The man grasped his neck but there was no stemming the flow of blood that spurted from between his fingers. It seemed that rage and fury were the only things keeping him upright. Ozzie was sure he would have charged at her, or leaped for the gun, if it wasn't for the throaty growl reverberating from behind him.

Basheba and Buck circled the man, calm and calculating, patiently waiting for the right moment to strike. There was no order given. The two simply moved as one. A single being of raw brutality. Buck latched onto his hip, clamping down until the bone shattered. Basheba went for his neck again, wrapping her limbs around the man's flailing body, sinking her teeth into the soft flesh of his jugular. The man thrashed and screamed as much as his broken body would allow, but all the effort was for nothing. Together, Buck and Basheba brought him down, unrelenting in their attack until the man lay motionless beneath them.

Basheba rocked back onto her heels. Panting so hard her shoulders rocked with the motion, she tipped her blood-soaked face to the sky. Absently, she wiped the back of her forearm over her mouth, only managing to smear more blood onto her pale skin.

"Cadwyn, Ozzie, you might want to look away for a bit," she panted, absently wiping some sweat from her forehead, leaving a smear of blood behind.

The words shook Ozzie from his shock. All at once, everything crashed down upon him. The sight, the chaos, the coppery stench that now hung thick in the air. Bile surged up Ozzie's throat with enough force to double him over. He braced against his knees as he wretched, spewing the limited contents of his stomach on the ground between his feet. Sucking in a breath made him throw up again.

Cadwyn was instantly by his side, one large hand rubbing his back in comforting circles. Ozzie barely straightened enough to catch a glimpse at the older man. It was enough to know he wasn't the only one sick to his stomach. Neither one of them were prepared for Basheba's sudden gasp of horror.

"What is it?" Cadwyn asked.

Looking out from under his eyelashes, Ozzie watched Basheba hurriedly patting her chest, each touch leaving a streak of blood on her flannel shirt.

"Basheba?" Mina asked.

"He broke the chain," Basheba gasped. She threw herself onto the ground, frantically clawing at the earth, blindly searching for something, her body violently trembling.

Mina took a step into the meadow. "Basheba?"

The blonde's trembling only grew worse as she began to pluck unseen items from the layer of matted leaves. Ozzie didn't get a chance to see what they were as the frantic girl cradled each one protectively to her stomach. Mina glanced at them, as if checking to see if either one of them was willing to take her place, but neither was in a condition to do so.

"Basheba, what's wrong? Maybe I can help."

"The rings," Basheba said, her voice cracking with tears, the words tumbling over each other. "There're twenty-six wedding rings. I need to find them. He broke the chain!"

The last words were spat out like a snarl, filled with enough rage that she paused her searching to kick wildly at the corpse beside her. They could hear her counting, over and over, the numbers increasing each time, but never reaching twenty-six.

"The Claddagh ring," Basheba muttered between heavy breaths.

By this point, she had gouged a deep groove into the soft earth, leaving clogs of dirt sticking to the layer of blood.

"The Irish Claddagh," she whispered. "I have to find it. Mom said I needed to take care of it. I can't lose it. She'd be so disappointed."

Mina crossed the last of the separating distance and knelt down before her. Concerned, Buck whimpered, nuzzling at his mistress's side in an attempt to get her attention. It was the first time Ozzie had ever seen Basheba ignore his attempts. All of her attention was fixed on the search for the missing ring. It was only disturbed by her compulsive need to recount the ones in her hand.

"It's okay," Mina whispered.

"It's not okay!" Basheba all but screamed. "That ring is all that's left. They took everything else!" Hyperventilating, she resumed her search, muttering over and over that she had promised her mother that she'd take care of it.

Moving carefully, as if worried any sudden movement would provoke Basheba's wrath, Mina reached into a clump of moss and plucked free a small loop that glistened in the light. Basheba froze. Suddenly, the blonde burst forward, wrapping a very startled Mina in a tight hug. Giggles broke the tension. At least enough that Ozzie was able to straighten somewhat, so long as he only breathed through his mouth.

"Thank you," Basheba grinned, the coating of blood making the sight grotesque.

She snatched up the ring and hurriedly counted her collection.

"Twenty-six," she breathed.

All tension instantly left her body as she slumped down against Buck, at last giving the dog the attention he craved. They cuddled together, a cozy image of gore, as Basheba's giggles became mixed with sobs.

"Twenty-six."

"Basheba," Mina said gently. She waited patiently for Basheba to quieten.

With a snort, the blonde tried to wipe the tears from her eyes, but only succeeded in covering the last patches of clear skin with gore.

"We need to go," Mina said. "Can you lead the way?"

Basheba sniffed, blinking her water-logged eyes. "Yeah," she breathed. Like a flash of lightning, the raw grief vanished, and she straightened. She eyed the corpse. "We'll have to wrap up the leftovers. I've got a thermal blanket in Buck's armor."

"What?" Mina asked, subtly checking with the boys.

Cadwyn looked as baffled as her.

"Well, we need to take at least one of them," Basheba said. Carefully, she stored all the rings in her pocket, shoving them down until there was no chance of them slipping out. Then she retrieved the folded thermal blanket from Buck and tossed it to Mina.

"What's this for?" Mina asked.

"Whichever body you pick, we're going to have to keep it warm," Basheba replied, hurrying to retrieve her knife while seemingly keeping the booby trap in place.

Mina glanced from the thermal blanket in her hands to the bodies scattered around the meadow. "Why do we need them warm?" Mina asked.

"Because it's past sundown and we have to go through its territory," Basheba replied. "We're not getting past it without a distraction and the only thing that distracts it is human flesh. So, pick a corpse, or offer up a limb."

Once more, Mina looked to the boys. Ozzie wished there was some measure of comfort he could offer. In the end, he couldn't even bring himself to help wrap up the man's body.

CHAPTER 16

A strange silence filled Mina's head, as if all of her competing thoughts had somehow combined to create an all-consuming white noise. She followed beside Basheba, her fingers aching from carrying the dead weight for so long. In the end, it had taken all four of them to carry the makeshift body bag over the uneven earth. There had been little discussion amongst the group once they had set out, as if everyone had assumed that Basheba would instinctually know the way. The silence of the mob faded away, replaced by their soft, shuffling footsteps and the distant bubbling of a stream. Basheba angled them toward it.

Mina bit her tongue as she trudged along. *Organize your thoughts,* she told herself. *Plan it out.* Even now, she clung to the scientific method like a talisman against evil. It was her only way to organize and understand the world around her. Experience had taught her well to be careful of how she approached Basheba. By now, she knew the smartest course of action was not to voice her questions at all. Unfortunately, she also knew it wasn't her nature. Especially not now that her entire world order was crumbling down upon her head.

Dad knew. The single whisper slashed to the forefront of her mind, bringing with it a wave of sickening vertigo. Her father and mother had been the very foundation of her life. Everything she was, everything she thought, was built upon the unshakable knowledge that they always had her best interests at heart. Anyone else could be wrong. Everything else could change. But their love and regard for her were set like stone. She saw herself through their eyes, and had structured her entire personality to match. *And it was all a lie. They never believed in me. Never thought me destined for great things.*

Mina eyed Basheba out of the corner of her eyes, sick with the growing suspicion that the blonde might have been right about her. That she was nothing more than a pampered little princess with no understanding of the world around her.

Whitney's voice taunted her from her memories. *You'll never understand, little princess. Let's get you back to your daddy.* The woods opened up, revealing a narrow stream that glistened in the moonlight. It filled the warm night air with the clean note of fresh water and musky moss.

"Okay," Basheba said, her voice soft enough to blend in with the silence rather than disturb it. "Five-minute break."

She dropped her corner of the body bag, the jerk forcing the material from Mina's grasp. The corpse hit the ground with a dull thud. Not much of a noise, all things considered, but it made Mina cringe all the same. Basheba was in good spirits and she spun around and threw a smile in Cadwyn's direction.

"Need help with your leg?"

Cadwyn swallowed thickly, his eyes a little too wide, and the tendons in his neck pressing against the skin.

"Did you have to use your teeth?" he asked, the question almost making him gag.

"It wasn't exactly a planned thing," Basheba protested. "If it helps, I didn't even chip a tooth."

Cadwyn drew in a deep breath through his nose. "Actually, that does help a little."

"But still incredibly gross?"

"If that's your nice way of saying utterly horrific."

"You handle blood on every other part of the human body," she pointed out.

"And you handle kids swarming around Disneyland. Wanna babysit?"

Basheba jerked a thumb over her shoulder, "I'll go wash my mouth out."

"I would appreciate it," Cadwyn said, still keeping his distance.

It looked as if every joint in his body was locked in place with tension.

Ozzie gagged and avoided all eye contact. "Thanks."

"I didn't lose any teeth, if that helps," Basheba said.

"It does," Cadwyn said softly.

Absently, he ran his tongue over his teeth. Mina had the sneaking suspicion he was counting them. *He was just a kid,* Mina thought. Images came unbidden to her mind's eye, of a lanky little pre-teen trapped under a demon, helpless as the monster pulled his teeth out one-by-one.

His brother was possessed. The thought sent a shiver down her spine. *Did the demon wear his brother's skin while he hurt him?* Squeezing her eyes shut, Mina forced the thought away in favor of focusing on the more pressing issue. Namely, she was now in a haunted wood with a woman who had quite literally ripped a man's throat out with her teeth. But first, she carefully watched Cadwyn for a moment.

He dropped the body with the bare minimum of care, just enough to be considered respectful, and shuffled to one of the larger boulders that speckled the riverbed. Ozzie trailed beside him, jittery with unspent adrenaline and his eyes constantly searching the tree line. Basheba picked a spot by a rocky outcrop rather than the stream itself. Even by the moonlight, Mina could see she was cleaning the blood off more with mud than with water. The sight brushed aside Mina's thoughts enough to recall, *she's terrified of water.*

Basheba's namesake had been one of the small children that had brought the Witch to the noose. One of the first to be tormented by the vengeful ghost. *And for all she survived, she drowned in a few inches of water.* During their last visit, the Witch had left no doubt that she was well aware of Basheba's fear. If it hadn't been for Buck and Ozzie, Basheba would have drowned in the very same river her ancestor had died in. *And I did nothing.* Mina curled her arms around herself, forcing herself to endure the wave of shame that crashed down upon her, and all the memories that still haunted her nightmares.

Icy water rolled against her skin. The buzz of the bee swarm covered every sound. She closed her eyes and could still see the hive that had hollowed out the hanging man. All of her life, she had heard of what it was like to be terrified. None of it had prepared her for the soul-shattering actuality of the emotion. Or how she would react to it. *I just froze.*

Mina snapped her eyes open and drew a deep breath into her lungs. *Crying about it isn't going to change anything.* The words were an echoing memory of her own, spoken gently by her parents, more as a comfort than a chastisement. Her gut hurt just to think about them. And how her relationship with them was never going to be the same. She hadn't realized she had once again fallen into self-pity until she heard her mother click her tongue. *Mina, whatever you're looking for isn't going to be on your shoes. Chin up.* Her spine straightened without her conscious decision and she strode over to Basheba.

"Can we talk?" she asked as she approached, not wanting to startle her. "I have a few questions."

The silence that followed the request highlighted how much chatter had been going on before. Basheba paused, a handful of mud cupped in her hand and a rattlesnake smile curling the corners of her mouth.

"I'm not trying to be provocative," Mina said in a rush.

Shadows robbed Basheba's eyes of their blue shine, but not their intensity. "What are you trying for, exactly?"

"An education."

Basheba's eyebrow jumped up her mud streaked forehead. Mina bit her bottom lip hard, forcing her eyes to remain on Basheba. *Chin up.*

"I know we don't get along."

"What?" Basheba drew the word out mockingly.

"But you've always been honest with me. Brutally so." Mina huffed a small laugh when the truth of her next words sunk in. "You're the only one I can trust to be unequivocally honest with me."

After a moment of contemplation, Basheba seemed pleased by the words.

"All right, little princess. We've got a few minutes to kill while Cadwyn patches himself up. What do you want to know?"

"Everything," Mina said. "But I think we should start with more pressing matters."

"Makes sense."

"Why is Isaac so afraid? What did you do?"

Basheba barked a laugh. "And here I thought you were going to ask about *it*."

"Yes, that's important," Mina admitted. "But I trust that you have that well in hand. I need to think about what comes after."

"And my uncle comes after?"

Mina's eyes lowered despite her best efforts. "My father hinted that he knew some things about Isaac's relationship with the cult. I don't know to what extent. But..."

"But he made it clear he was in Isaac's corner?" Basheba finished for her.

"Yes," Mina mumbled.

She wasn't sure how she expected Basheba to react. Laughter wasn't it.

"Yeah, that sounds about right. You know, my great aunt used to say that, when people are scared, they cling to their status quo. Unfortunately for us, Katrina came along in a pretty bad time for women. And our families haven't moved on from there. Not really. They put on airs, say the right things, and swear up and down that they consider women their equals. But apply a little pressure and, well, they run back to their status quo."

"My father's not like that," Mina said on reflex.

The moment the words left her mouth, she found herself questioning them. She flinched when Basheba's smile turned into sweet poison.

"Isn't he?"

"He's always taken care of me." Mina's voice softened with each

163

word as her doubt grew.

"Wow, your education is seriously lacking. Let me impart some wisdom my momma taught me." Her smile fell, her face became relaxed, but her eyes retained their fire. "Only weak men seek to control strong women. And strong women will never bow to weak men."

Mina bristled at the not so subtle jab against her mother but held her tongue on that account.

"Did Isaac try to make you bow?" Mina shifted under Basheba's gaze. "I just want to know what war zone I walked into."

"Fair enough."

"Really?" Mina asked.

"You're right. This does concern you now, so you might as well be in on it," Basheba said. She took to playfully tussling Buck as she spoke. "The Allaway line has a lot of traditions. Some even regarding a girl's first period. I got a party. Complete with cake, a pearl necklace, and an octopus hairpin."

"An octopus hairpin?" Ozzie said, puzzled.

"A kraken. They're the unofficial family sigil. The pin was the kind that sits on the back of your head. And you thread a sharp little barb through its tangled tentacles to keep it in place." Her gaze grew unfocused as her memories dragged her under. She pulled herself from them violently. "The Bells had their own tradition regarding periods. You're officially a woman, so you better start popping out the crotch-goblins. Only Isaac still believed that when I came around. And he was very vocal about my responsibilities and obligations."

Cadwyn made a disgusted sound. "You would have been, what? Twelve?"

"Nine, I was an early bloomer."

"And he was talking about babies?" Ozzie squeaked. "That's gross."

Basheba smirked, "You should have seen his face when I told him that I had no intention of *ever* having a child."

Mina almost smiled at that, recalling how frightened the blonde was of children. It may have come across as disgust, but it was terror.

"And that's why you're at odds?" Mina asked.

"No, this is the background necessary to understand how we got where we are. Just shut up for a few more minutes," Basheba said. "Where was I? Oh, right, my period party. The next day, we got word that Claudia was sick. No one knew what was wrong with her, but Isaac was beside himself and begging my parents to meet him at the hospital. It was all last minute. My sisters got to stay with some friends and my brother and I were left at home."

"Your parents left two children home alone?" Mina asked.

"We were independent kids," Basheba dismissed.

Buck playfully chewed on her hand. Mina suspected it was the only thing keeping her from slipping into her memories.

"It was the first time we had a home to be left in. We built it ourselves. This little one-room log cabin in the Alaskan wilderness." She bit her bottom lip to keep in a chuckle. "No running water. No heat. No electricity. No neighbors for miles. We had grizzly bears and moose cutting through our front yard and, in the winter, I used the aurora as my nightlight. Heaven couldn't be more beautiful."

"How do you use the restroom if there's no running water?" Ozzie whispered to Cadwyn only to be shushed.

"My brother used to love to fish. We spent the whole day on the frozen lake before we were forced inside by an approaching snowstorm. I remember going to sleep with him making shadow puppets on the walls." Her smile fell. "I woke up with a stranger looming over me. He smelt like sour milk and had the roughest hands. They felt like sandpaper against my skin. One clamped over my mouth, the other pulled at my clothes."

Mina's stomach rolled with dread and disgust. *Nine, she was only nine.*

"He hurt you?" Cadwyn whispered when Basheba fell silent.

She stirred. "Turns out my little hairpin was sharp enough to puncture a man's neck, if you swing it hard enough. I must've gotten the artery because he bled out on top of me. It took both me and my brother to shove him off."

"Basheba, I'm so sorry that happened to you," Mina said. "But I don't understand."

Basheba paused; Buck grumbled at the sudden loss of attention. "Is it really that hard for you to think that family could turn on family?"

"Isaac sent him after you?" Cadwyn asked, his voice taking on a deep growl.

"Them, Cadwyn. He sent *them* after me."

"I don't understand," Mina repeated.

"It was the third guy who was too much of an idiot to cover his tracks properly," Basheba continued. "He had printed out the webpage. Can you believe that? Looking back, that guy's death was just natural selection at work. I'll spare the minor of the group the gory details. Just think of it as an advertisement. Calling all creeps, there's a little girl alone in the woods. Do what you want with her."

"Isaac tried to have you killed?" Cadwyn asked.

"Worse," Basheba said, pulling Buck closer for a hug, careful of the spikes that covered them both. "The only restriction was that I was to be left alive. Well, alive enough to bring the resulting child to term." A bitter laugh cracked out of her. "And before you ask how I know it was him. Only Isaac is stupid enough to think my parents would force their underage daughter to give birth to her rapist's kid. Honestly, I don't know what he thought would happen. It's bothered me for years. All I can think is that he was hoping I'd be too mortified to tell my parents about the assault. That I'd keep it a secret until it was too late for an abortion."

"Oh, my God," Mina whispered, her arms wrapping around her torso.

Basheba scoffed. "Yeah, he's always hated me. Way more than any of my siblings. I mean, he never tried anything like that with them, or anyone else, as far as I've heard. I don't know what I did to tick him off so much. Admittedly, it probably didn't help that I cussed him out with a rather extensive vocabulary when he presumed he had a say over my womb."

"What did your parents think happened?" Ozzie asked. "I mean, how did you explain away the dead bodies?"

Basheba laughed, good-natured and warm. "I was nine. Mom had long since taught us how to hide a dead body."

Mina's brow furrowed. The confusion increasing when she noticed how baffled Cadwyn was. *It's not a skill taught to the four families.*

"Why did she teach you that?" Mina ventured.

"Tradition," Basheba said with a small, secretive smile. "Anyway, after the first couple, my brother and I took the fight outside. It was the two of us and the Alaskan wilderness against some morons who couldn't track an elephant. They never stood a chance against us," she chuckled, her eyes softening. "*Us.* That's how my brother always worded it. He never put the blame on me. It didn't matter how they came at us. He never wavered."

Basheba released Buck only long enough to wipe at her cheeks.

"You never told anyone?" Cadwyn asked.

A look of horror twisted up her face. "And have my father find out? I couldn't do that to him. My dad was a good man. It wasn't his fault we share DNA with the human equivalent of a stomach flu. And I'd be damned if I let him suffer for it." Shaking her head, she stared off into the distance. "I decided Isaac and I would sort it out ourselves, when the time was right."

"So, when you said that you'd do to him what you did to the others..." Mina prompted.

Basheba flashed her bloodied teeth. "Yeah, Ozzie's still too innocent to hear any of that in detail. And, honestly, I still don't entirely trust your law and order mentality. There's no statute of limitations on murder, after all."

"Who would believe me?" Mina asked, trying to keep her words light.

Basheba took the words as intended and smiled. "I've got that working for me at least."

"So, let me get this straight," Mina thought aloud. "From his perspective, he sets you up. Probably expecting a frantic call from two scared kids. But that doesn't happen. You and your brother never say anything, and he can't bring up the subject to see what happened."

"Isaac had the good sense to avoid direct conflict with either of my parents," Basheba said, once more curling up with Buck. "They both intimidated the hell out of him."

"And that's why he's so aggravated," Mina murmured with sudden realization.

She glanced around only to see confused frowns.

"I'm starting to get an idea of the way Isaac thinks, and I'm sickened to realize we have something in common. We're both planners."

Basheba cocked an eyebrow.

"I didn't say we were *good* at planning," Mina clarified, physically sick by the truth in the words she spoke. "Just that, it's what we do. We overthink things. And that can lead to a lot of mistakes, especially if we start with a misapprehension."

"He mistook Basheba's silence for fear," Cadwyn offered, still somewhat apprehensive to follow where Mina led.

"He assumed he would have Basheba's backing as soon as he took his place as head of the household. And, with her, he'd have all the things he doesn't have amongst the four families."

Basheba lifted her hand and waved it to get attention. "What's that? I'm not exactly popular."

"But you are respected." Cadwyn added with a smirk, "Sometimes, grudgingly so."

"My parents outright detest you, and even they admit you're the best at this," Mina said.

Ozzie followed Basheba's example and lifted his hand. "Percival actually thinks the world of you."

"Aw, that's sweet," Basheba preened.

"My theory is that Isaac watched you earn respect and influence, and he built his plans around the assumption that, one day, that would be his own," Mina continued, absently tapping the ends of her hair against her lower lip as she thought. "But I think Whitney is in charge of the cult, now."

"Oh, so *now* it's a cult," Basheba muttered under her breath.

It was easy enough for Mina to ignore the comment as her mind raced.

"I overheard them discussing a deal they had with Isaac. And my dad suggested that Isaac has worked hard to come to an arrangement with them." She rushed on as all three of her listeners perked up at that information. "I'm thinking he was using Basheba as leverage. Perhaps threatening to unleash her on the town."

"Unleash me? I'm not an animal."

"You did blow up a morgue, and you carpeted the town with poisonous gas," Cadwyn deadpanned.

"The minotaur started it," Basheba protested.

"You threatened to set them on fire," Ozzie said.

The blonde huffed. "That was *hours* ago. Stop living in the past."

"You gutted two men," Mina noted absently. "And ripped someone's throat out with your *teeth*."

Basheba's mouth opened and closed a few times. "Yeah, okay, you got me there."

"If Isaac overplayed his hand, Basheba's behavior would risk everything. He's supposedly head of the family. If he can't get her in line, then everyone will see him for what he is."

"A weak, petty man," Basheba noted.

"He'd be desperate to prove he has power over you. Killing you might be the only way he has left to do that."

Ozzie meekly put up his hand again. "I don't mean to sound like a jerk, but why is any of this relevant? I mean, relevant *right now*?"

"Because my father made it clear, in no uncertain terms, that he agrees with Isaac," Mina said. "I don't know if he's aware just how deep Isaac's sunk, but the situation concerns me. Not to mention all the spy implications."

"Spy implications?" Ozzie said, barely suppressing his amusement.

"The families talk amongst themselves, right?" Mina asked.

Cadwyn looked as if he had just been struck. His hands paused as he packed away his med-kit. "There is an unofficial council of family elders."

"And I'm guessing they'll all talk rather freely," Mina said. "I don't feel easy knowing every family secret can work its way back to the cult, if not to the Witch herself."

"Is that how she knew how to find me?" Ozzie asked.

Cadwyn patted his shoulder in an offer of comfort but didn't say anything, leaving the question hanging over the group.

"In the spirit of full disclosure," Mina continued awkwardly, not sure how Basheba would respond, "when I received my music box, my parents both assured me they would 'fix' it. Before anyone jumps to conclusions, I have no evidence that *anyone* can sway the Witch's Harvest selection."

"But you think he can?" Even as Basheba carefully stripped all emotion from her words, she couldn't hide the spark of fire burning within the question.

"I have a habit of overestimating my father," Mina replied. "And I'd like to point out, if Isaac has somehow wormed his way into a position where he can have that power, my father wouldn't be the only one he's pimped it out to."

"He set my father up to die," Basheba snarled. "He's choosing who gets to be the human sacrifice."

"We don't know that for sure," Cadwyn said, swiftly adding, "but the possibility is enough to worry me. I'll look into it once we get back."

"I can ask Percival," Ozzie offered. "I know I can trust him with my life. And he's made it pretty clear he thinks Isaac is a creep."

"I love your dad," Basheba grinned.

"Don't worry, I won't tell him anything you've told us."

Basheba chuckled. "I'm actually kinda hoping you'll tell a lot of people. I've always told myself I'll hold this truce so long as dad's alive and Isaac keeps to himself. Now, he's actively tried to kill me. So, I'm going to burn his entire world down around him. You know, when I have a free five minutes. Speaking of time restraints, we should get moving. That thing," she said as she jabbed a finger toward the corpse Mina had blissfully forgotten about for fifteen minutes, "is going to draw *its* attention. We want to keep moving."

Chapter 17

Basheba kept a close eye on Buck as they made their way over the uneven forest floor. The thick blanket of wildflowers masked the steadily increasing slope. Basheba's legs throbbed and her arms trembled from carrying the weight for so long. *Why are dead people always so heavy? It's just so inconsiderate.* As the hours stretched on, she was forced to confront the fact that she was the smallest, weakest one within the group. This made her all the more determined to outlast the others. She would be damned if she was the first one to ask to rest.

They struggled to the top of the precipice and awkwardly began to shuffle down the other side. Buck trotted on before them, idly sniffing at everything within reach. Basheba tripped more than once by not looking where she was going, but still didn't take her eyes off of Buck. He would be the first one to know *it* had found them.

Conversation had dwindled soon after they had started off. Whatever curiosity they had dwindled under their growing anxiety. Paranoia hung thick in the floral drenched air. The night encased them, with only their own footsteps and the stray hoot of an owl to disturb it. By the moon peeking through the canopy, Basheba estimated it was past midnight when Mina couldn't keep her mouth shut any longer.

"What is *it*?"

Much to Basheba's relief, Ozzie took that as a cue that they were stopping and dumped his portion of the bag. Cadwyn followed suit and promptly slumped his weight against the nearest tree.

"There's been a lot of speculation over the years," Basheba said. "*It's* the reason we go through the hiking trail's parking lot."

Mina huffed slightly, pulling her arms over her chest to release some of the knots in her muscles. "That doesn't tell me much."

"You don't know enough about cryptozoology for it to make any sense," Basheba countered.

"I'm sure you're up for the challenge of explaining."

Basheba smirked, oddly amused. *She might actually be tolerable if she got her ego under control.*

"Personally," Basheba said, "I always thought of it as a *Mahaha*."

Ozzie perked up. "Did you just fake laugh?"

"No, that's what it's called," Basheba said.

His dark brows knitted with suspicion. "I might not be able to see the punchline, but I know this is a setup."

"The *Mahaha* is a creature of ancient Inuit legend," Basheba said.

"It's a monster that tickles you to death," Cadwyn said cautiously, as if dredging up a distant memory.

"Look at that, Mr. Winthrop, you finally managed to impress me," Basheba said.

"I've saved your life on numerous occasions."

"Yeah, but you're a nurse," she teased. "That's not impressive, that's just being competent."

"I'm sorry," Mina cut in. "It *tickles* you to death? How is that intimidating?"

Basheba suppressed a shiver at the memories her mind's eye started to play like an old movie. Instinctively, she looked for Buck as she spoke.

"It has these ten-inch-long nails. Strong like silver. Sharp as a scalpel. You'll hear it before you see it. It giggles. I've never heard anything laugh like that. It's just..." She bit her lips, trying to steady her breathing. "Sadistic. Gleefully sadistic. I don't know how it works, but you'll laugh when it 'tickles' you. When its nails slice through your flesh like hot steel through soft butter. You'll laugh as it turns your stomach to mush. You'll be smiling while it eats you."

Jerking herself free from the past, she crouched down, whistling for Buck. He trotted over instantly, presenting his rump for a rub. Not an easy task, given his armor. The brush of his fur beneath her fingertips chased away the horrors of the past.

"Then why are we going this way?" Ozzie asked after a length of tense silence.

Basheba shrugged. "It's faster. If we can keep up the pace and cut across the river, we'll be there just after dawn."

"It takes three days from the hiking trail." Mina didn't say the words as an accusation or complaint. She spoke them with fear. "We willingly spend two extra days in the Witch Woods rather than face the *Mahaha*."

"That's why we've got our friend in tow." Basheba smiled, unable to resist giving the corpse a swift kick.

Despite her nonchalant tone, Basheba was already regretting staying in one place for so long. Being found by the monster was an inevitability. *Where* they came into contact was somewhat under their control. And she wanted to make sure that it was on the edges of his territory, not in the heart of it.

"Break's over," Basheba declared, giving Buck a parting rub.

Trained as he was, it didn't take more than that for him to return to his vigilant stance. The others were somewhat more reluctant to return to their task. Each one of them was now paying far more attention to the dark woods.

"Katrina knows we're here," Mina said.

Basheba scrunched up her face as she hefted the dead weight back onto her shoulder. Short as she was, she needed to hold it a lot higher simply to be level with the others.

"But she hasn't sent anything after us yet," Mina added, casting a quick glance at Basheba. "That's a lot of faith to put in her *Mahaha*. Is that faith earned?"

"I survived it," Basheba said.

The scars on her ribs burned with the memory, and she could taste the crisp river water that had saved her.

"How many didn't?" Mina asked.

Gripping the thermal sheet tighter, Basheba jerked forward, forcing the others into movement.

"Don't worry about it," Basheba said, adding under her breath, "so long as there's a body of water around."

"What?" Mina asked.

"You know, I love it when you're silent," Basheba smiled.

Mina took the not-so-subtle hint and turned her full focus to lugging the body forward. The wild bouquet grew thicker and higher. For the others, the flowing stalks brushed against their hips. Basheba's tiny stature allowed them up quite a bit higher, and the combined scents made her head spin. The tiny pink bulbs of bleeding hearts hooked on the buttons of Basheba's flannel shirt as they entered into a wide meadow. In the darkness, it took her a few moments to notice what other flowers were there to greet them. Stopping just on the precipice of the meadow, she dumped the weight, retrieved her phone, and swept the weak flashlight across the area.

"I'm going to need my bow," she muttered to Cadwyn, adrenaline flooding her veins.

The bow and quiver caught on his broad shoulders in his haste.

"I'm not intending to annoy you," Mina said.

"And yet you always manage to."

"Are you able to shoot that with any kind of accuracy?" Mina pressed on.

Basheba glared at her. "I'm a good hunter."

"I'm not questioning that," Mina said, waving a finger to indicate Basheba's eye patch. "I'm just thinking your depth perception might be a little off right now."

Not willing to admit that Mina had a point, she snipped, "I promise not to shoot you. Now, can I please focus on saving your life?"

Mina's expression hovered somewhere between satisfied, chastised, and irritated, but she nodded anyway.

"What's wrong?" Ozzie whispered.

Basheba risked sweeping the light once more over the meadow, annoyed to find that not one of them understood. Clenching her teeth against a frustrated groan, she elaborated.

"They're all warnings."

"The flowers?" Cadwyn asked.

Mina asked at the same time, "Warnings?"

"Ozzie's an arachnophobe and Cadwyn has a thing about teeth," Basheba said. "That purple one by your hand is called *spiderwort*. The little white ones are *toothwort*."

"I don't know much about flowers, but aren't they both native to Tennessee?" Cadwyn asked, inching closer to pass her the bow and quiver.

"They are," Basheba admitted. "But you see those ones a bit further in? The white ones that look like spiked-up corn cobs? That's *asphodel*. It's not supposed to be in these woods, and it means 'may regrets follow you to the grave.'"

She opened the quiver and fished her hand into the internal pocket to retrieve her hand guard.

"I can also see some *dog rose*, which means 'pleasure and pain.' And I'm not keen on these guys." She paused to pluck a stalk of tiny green cups. "*Bells of Ireland*." Basheba held it out for Cadwyn to take, a small smile on her lips.

"Bell," he said with an understanding nod.

She set the quiver in place and tugged until the strap was flush against her chest. It was awkward to put her backpack over the quiver, but she had grown used to the lopsided weight. "They also mean 'good luck.' Oh, and the whole meadow is surrounded by *witch elms*."

"I'm sorry," Mina said, clearly struggling to come to terms with everything she had just heard. "You know flower meanings? Really?"

"I like to know when someone's threatening me. And the woods are Katrina's preferred method of communication." She grudgingly added, "And I find it amusing when people thank me for giving them bouquets that passive-aggressively insult them."

"It's even harder to imagine you being *passive*-aggressive," Ozzie said, inching closer still to the group, his eyes restlessly searching the shadows.

Basheba smirked. "My parents were big on family unity. It forced us to be creative in ways to insult each other."

"My brother and I use colors as swear words," Mina said.

Basheba studied her out of the corner of her eye, her face mostly hidden in shadows. "Well, peach. Let's go fuchsia up Katrina's day."

The thick leather of her hand guard quickly warmed to her skin. Well used, it now fit her fingers and wrist like a second skin, making it easy to notch the end of her arrow into the bow. A low series of whistles brought Buck around, commanding him to be prepared and alert. She gave the others time enough to organize the dead weight between them and began to lead the way into the meadow.

"Can't we go around?" Ozzie asked.

"I'm not keen to see what's waiting for us in the shadows," she whispered back. "If they want us, they can come out into the open and get us."

There was nothing to gain from informing the poor boy that Katrina loved to act as if the trees had been named after her. Or from letting him know about any of the things Basheba had found nestled in the clustered needles that consumed their trunks. *Let him keep some measure of innocence,* she thought.

The moon brightened as they moved, letting the shadows deepen until its light almost seemed to die just beyond the tree line. Basheba kept her steps light, and her hands ready upon the bow, her gaze snapping toward every trace of movement. A cool breeze came out of nowhere to rustle the trees and towering flowers. Basheba hunched low, almost completely hidden by the shifting petals. Behind her, the others followed suit as best they could, barely able to keep from dropping the corpse.

Buck's growl rumbled through the sudden silence of the woods. His lips pulled back from his fangs as his gaze became locked on a spot just to their right. Readjusting her grip on the bowstring and arrow, she tracked her pet's line of sight. Moonlight flared into an unnatural silver glare that all but destroyed her night vision. Cursing under her breath, she narrowed her eyes, peering through the dancing flowers.

Ethereal strips of ivory pushed against the darkness before disappearing once more out of sight. Under her watchful gaze, another path of the illusive white emerged like a shark from the ocean's depths, stretching out to form a gigantic smile. Basheba moved on reflex. Flower petals scattered in the wake of the arrow, carving a path across the field. The journey barely took a second. Still, the smile disappeared long before the arrow struck home, leaving the shaft to be swallowed by the darkness.

"Damn it," Basheba hissed, readjusting her displaced eye patch.

Low, giggling laughter drifted on the night air, swirling around them, brushing against the back of her neck like tickling fingers. The sound had echoed through her nightmares for years and yet she still reacted to it like the first time. Swallowing hard, she tried to force her heart out of her throat and retrieved another arrow. Lowering her weight onto one shin allowed her to completely hide within the wildflowers. The laughter returned. Louder than before and rolling like mist.

"Stalk," she whispered to Buck.

Instantly, his nose went into the air. Almost immediately, he had the scent, and he whirled to the left. There wasn't a drop of bloodhound in him, but his paw went up all the same. A clear and decisive point. Sliding across the damp earth, Basheba positioned her bow over Buck's outstretched paw and fired. The swaying plants swallowed the arrow almost instantaneously.

"Did you hit it?" Ozzie asked.

"You can see more than I can, Ozzie," she hissed, already getting to her feet, a new arrow in hand. She turned to find them all just staring at her. "Now's the time we run."

Cadwyn gripped the body's wrist, pulling it free of the bag to hurl the dead weight over his shoulders. The heavy weight almost dragged him down. Sheer determination allowed him to straighten. With clenched teeth, he commanded Ozzie and Mina to run. They followed the order without question. Basheba settled herself between the two teenagers and Cadwyn, an arrow at the ready and Buck by her side.

The laughter returned. As if every blade of grass and suspended leaf carried the sound. Buck kept his nose high, sniffing the air, searching to catch the scent again. Suddenly, Buck locked his legs. His claws ripped up chunks of dirt as he slid to a stop, head lowered, teeth bared, and one paw outstretched before him. Once more, Basheba dropped to one knee and fired blind. The laughter rose into a shrill delirium. The petals shattered to release a man into the air. Gravity didn't hinder him. Arms and legs rose as he loomed over her, his long talons glistening, shark-like teeth cutting down from his parted lips. Basheba fell onto her back, grappling for another arrow.

Buck streaked across her vision. A creature of ebony and fury. He sunk his teeth into the *Mahaha's* arm. Pure fear crashed through Basheba as she watched the deadly talons sweep down toward Buck. Forgoing the arrow, she cupped the bow with both hands and swung it like a bat into the *Mahaha's* haggard legs. The metal cracked against bone and the *Mahaha* stumbled back into the flowers. Basheba was on her feet before Cadwyn could try to help. He shifted the heavy weight across his shoulders, freeing one hand to place it against her back.

"Are you okay?"

"Yeah," she whispered.

Ozzie called to them, sharp and panicked, and she realized the teenagers had already made it to the tree line. Still, she refused to move until Buck responded to her sharp whistle. Pulling another arrow free, she knocked it and began to run. Even with the weight bearing down upon his shoulders, she knew Cadwyn could have easily taken the lead. Instead, he remained in step with her, refusing to leave her behind. *Noble, but stupid.*

The flowers slashed and swayed in two clear trails. A telltale sign of two creatures carving their way through the underbrush. Laughter bounced around the meadow, rolling over itself to grow into a deafening roar. Panting hard, Basheba forced another whistle. Buck barked as he emerged from the crush, a dark, undefinable shape closing in behind him. The other trail picked up speed as it bore down upon the two unprotected teenagers.

"Drop it," Basheba ordered.

Cadwyn tossed the corpse onto the ground, the impact resounding with a heavy thud. Basheba whirled on the body, her free hand tugging her hunting knife free.

"Hey!" she screamed as she drove the knife into the body's gut.

A sharp slice, a solid stomp, and the stench of cooling blood burst into the air. The trailing creature stopped short. Without the movement, it was impossible to tell where the giggling *Mahaha* was. Blood soaked her once more as she reached in and cut free the first organ her fingertips found.

"Basheba?" Cadwyn whispered.

She handed him her hunting knife, using her now-free hands to stab the kidney onto an arrow, hefting it to hurriedly judge the added weight. Behind her, Cadwyn flipped the knife in his hand with surprising skill, readjusting his grip to the back of the knife, so that the blade ran down the length of his forearm.

The breeze died to leave the coppery stench of blood pooling around them. All trace of movement stilled. Basheba licked her lips and glanced over her shoulder to meet Cadwyn's gaze. He nodded once, wordlessly agreeing to follow wherever she would lead him. *Hopefully, it's not to the grave.* The thought came before she could completely lock her emotions down. Silence lingered.

"Grab some of the organs," she instructed Cadwyn in a whisper before she called out, "Buck! Clear 'em out!"

Duck hunting had solidified the command. His snarls shattered the silence. The grass thrashed wildly, two trails cutting back and forth, entwining around each other and leaving no way to tell which was which.

"Come on, Buck," she whispered, her heart hammering against her chest.

Anxiety sparked under her skin, trying to make her restless. She forced her body to become stone, ready and alert, waiting for Buck to flush the *Mahaha* out. A streak of black bounded through the moon-drenched meadow. Half a heartbeat later, the sickly gray monster followed. Basheba seized the opportunity, angling the bow slightly higher to compensate for the weight of the organ. The bowstring snapped taut, hurling the arrow across the space. The *Mahaha* snapped a hand up, catching the arrow before the point could penetrate its flesh. But the allure of the organ was too enticing for it to ignore and it began to gnaw on the piece.

"Now," Basheba said.

They broke into a sprint. Plants crushed under their feet, pummeled into the soft earth. The wind picked up, howling through the witch elms to create a ghastly wailing howl. Mina screamed for them to hurry as Ozzie restlessly squirmed beside her.

"Cross the river!" Basheba bellowed.

Mina nodded, grabbed Ozzie with both hands, and dragged him away. Buck growled even as he sprinted, frothing at the mouth and hackles raised. Needing no instruction, Cadwyn scattered the organs with wide sweeps of his arm. Each bloody clump of flesh landed with a wet thud; a sound that was met with a rustle of reeds. They were short distractions that offered them only a few extra seconds. Both Basheba and Cadwyn exploited them all as best they could, running until their legs ached and their lungs were replaced with burning coals.

Laughter followed them, broken on occasion by the slick squelch of teeth ripping into raw meat. But each time it returned, it was closer than before, trailing behind them as if it were a game. Cadwyn quickened his pace, his long legs making it an easy task, and entered the forest first. He slowed just beyond the first twisted branches, catching his breath and frantically searching.

Without enough air to speak, Basheba shoved him with both

hands, forcing him to move. The clustered trees made it nearly impossible for them to travel side by side. If it wasn't for Cadwyn's remarkable skill at finding openings within the foliage, they would have been forced to travel single file. Buck leaped over a fallen log and plowed through the leaves, leading the way as he hunted the others down.

Basheba's backpack slapped against her spine. Sweat made her hand slip over her bow's handgrip. Her eyepatch, slicked with her body heat and sweat, shifted and itched against her skin. Still, she kept running, keeping Cadwyn in her peripheral vision and tracking the destruction of Buck's pursuit. She ran until her legs wobbled and she staggered to the side.

Without warning, the trees she relied on for support disappeared, leaving her grasping at air. The laughter had covered the sounds of the river. Basheba locked her knees, trying to slide to a stop before she toppled into the small ravine. She clawed at the rocky surface, her legs dangling over the edge, the damp moss soaking her jeans.

"Basheba!" Ozzie called from the other side of the riverbank. The froth of the rapids would have hidden him completely if it wasn't for the way he waved both of his arms.

Cadwyn didn't see the edge, either. But he threw himself into the fall, leaping forward as far as he could as ivory nails closed in around him. The wide sweep of the *Mahaha's* arms slashed through the night air. Blood splattered from the deadly tips as the *Mahaha* tightened its grip, narrowly missing its prey as Cadwyn dove into the river. The monster's nails created sparks against the stones as it dropped onto all fours to watch Cadwyn fall. It laughed until the moment he hit the water and disappeared into the rapids. Then it turned its burning eyes onto Basheba.

Basheba scrambled onto her feet to leap over the side, hoping to clear the rocks that clung to the bank. Razors slashed her torso, effortlessly cutting one strap of her bag. The current took her the second she hit the water. Battered against the stones and desperate for air, she could do little against the tide. She clawed at the moss drenched boulders. Her backpack slipped from her shoulders and was lost to the waves. She refused to lose her bow, too.

Basheba's breath was forced out of her lungs as the river's current crashed her into a boulder. She dragged herself up, gasping and sputtering, and bodily hugged the rock. Rushing water crushed her against unmoving stone and dulled her senses. Relief left her weak when she spotted Cadwyn crawling his way out onto the far bank, Buck huffing as he tugged at the half-drowned man. A surge of water rushed over her, a black wall that filled her with terror and dragged her down once more.

CHAPTER 18

Cadwyn's feet sunk into the mud as he dragged Basheba's motionless body out of the river. Buck pushed past him to nuzzle her hand and gently chew on her fingertips. She didn't respond. Whimpering anxiously, the large dog nudged her head, the spikes of his helmet scraping her skin. The river had taken her eyepatch, leaving the livid bruise on full display. It appeared stark against her pale skin.

"Is she breathing?" Ozzie gasped, half failing in his attempt to help get her out of the water.

Cadwyn dragged Basheba into his arms and hiked past the rattled teenagers, seeking out solid ground.

"I need some light," he snapped.

Mina could only gape at him, "The water ruined all of our phones."

Spotting a rock in the dim moonlight, he hurried to it, ordering Mina to untangle the limp girl from the bowstring and quiver.

"Where's her bag?" Ozzie asked somewhat breathlessly. "She never goes anywhere without it."

"She's bleeding," Mina noted.

Cadwyn ignored them both as he gently laid Basheba out on the stone. His hand went to the ever-present medical-kit he so obsessively carried everywhere. The familiar weight reassured him that they had everything they needed. Buck braced his front paws on the stone and began to lick Basheba's face, growing desperate to get a reaction.

"Ozzie, take care of Buck. Mina," he said as he tossed his med-kit against her chest, "get ready."

Mina nodded rapidly, tugging on a pair of gloves while Ozzie strained to pull the massive Rottweiler away from his owner. Cadwyn placed the side of his head against Basheba's chest, willing himself to hear a heartbeat, a breath.

"Goddamn it, Basheba," he hissed through clenched teeth.

With well-practiced ease, he began chest compressions, rocking her tiny body with each push. *She can't drown,* he told himself. *After everything, she can't go out this way.* Memories mocked him. A thousand stories of her namesake. A little girl that defied a witch and died in a shallow brook. The thoughts scattered when he reached thirty compressions and focused on tipping her head back. All of his focus was on watching her chest rise and fall with his borrowed breaths. She didn't breathe on her own, so he repeated the compressions. Droplets of water beaded from his hair and dripped onto her face. She still didn't stir.

"Do you know CPR?" Cadwyn asked Mina, perhaps too sharply as he kept count in his head.

"Yes," she replied. "I'm here the second you need me."

Two more breaths. Still nothing. *Don't let her die like this!* his brain commanded.

"Come on, Basheba," he whispered. "For once in your life, don't be stubborn."

Two more breaths. Another round of compressions. Each second jabbed a knife into him. *Six minutes,* the treacherous voice whispered in the back of his head. *The brain starts to die after six minutes. How long was she in the water?* He dipped down, sealing his mouth over hers to fill her lungs again. The first gurgle caught him off guard.

"Basheba?" Mina asked.

Ozzie staggered forward, dragged by Buck's renewed determination. Cadwyn rolled Basheba onto her side, settling her into the recovery position as bone-cracking coughs rattled her body. River water pulsated out of her in steady gushes, far more than her lungs should have been capable of holding. She began to gag. The pale light revealed enough to see the color changing in her cheeks but not what was choking her.

Cadwyn hooked two fingers into her mouth. A squirming mass pressed against his fingertips. He jerked back as the first of the infant snakes squirmed past her lips. More and more followed until it seemed like hundreds of them came pouring from her mouth. Each one writhing against the others as Basheba's coughs vomited the reptiles onto the stone. The growing mass pushed out into the moonlight and he noticed the scale pattern—a tell-tale speckled cross band that even he could recognize.

"Cottonmouths!" He threw an arm out, urging the others back from the venomous snakes, hurriedly bundling Basheba into his arms.

Her constant choking made it nearly impossible to hold her in any stable position. The snakes continued to pour from her, a writhing puddle that glistened in the dying moonlight. Slithering out into the world with a determination that unsettled Cadwyn.

Cadwyn cautiously backed up, terrified that he would trip and bring them both into a sea of venom. The snakes followed them into the trees, slithering into the thick foliage and out of sight. Buck threw himself against Ozzie's hold, half-wild with the impulse to protect his clearly distressed Basheba.

Her first deep breath sounded like a death rattle. It left Cadwyn both relieved and concerned as he sought the high ground. There wasn't anywhere they could go where the snakes couldn't follow, if so inclined. Mina helped Cadwyn scramble up onto a boulder, Ozzie and Buck close behind. What little light peeking through the canopy created a haphazard pattern on the forest floor that was barely enough to see by. Basheba's pained gasps covered the soft sounds around them.

"Are there any more?" Cadwyn asked, trying to arrange her so he could see in her mouth.

Basheba cried out, short and sharp and laced with pain.

Cadwyn stilled, "Where does it hurt?"

"My ribs," she choked. "Buck?"

"Buck's fine. He's right here," Cadwyn assured as he lowered her to sit on the stone. With his adrenaline fading, he felt the pain in his leg for the first time. The spike of agony made him crumble the last of the distance, and they fell to the ground.

"Sorry," he grumbled, reaching for the soggy hem of her flannel shirt.

In his exhaustion, he was almost pushed from the rock entirely as Buck nudged past. Basheba expertly avoided the spikes of Buck's armor to draw him into a hug.

"Hey, beautiful." Basheba's voice rasped as if she had inhaled fire, but her smile was bright and full. Buck's entire hindquarters scattered about with his excitement. "Sorry I worried you. I'm all right."

"We're okay, too," Mina said, a smirk pulling at her lips and seeping into her voice.

"I was getting around to asking." Basheba coughed hard, gasped in pain, and added, "Don't be jealous."

Balling the shirt up at the side, Cadwyn spotted the scratch marks. Four clean slashes that thankfully didn't cut to the bone.

"Why does my chest hurt so much?" Basheba asked.

"It could be the CPR. You have to be a bit rough," Cadwyn said.

Ozzie loomed over his shoulder. "It could also be the ridiculous amount of snakes you just spewed."

"Snakes?" Basheba asked.

"It doesn't matter," Cadwyn said. "Let me tend to these."

"Do you need my shirt off?" Untangling herself from Buck, she quickly worked the line of buttons, opening the wet material without a hint of embarrassment.

Cadwyn released a grateful sigh. Having never seen Basheba bashful, he had no idea how to handle that particular scenario. Mina inched her way closer, his med-kit cradled between both hands, watching intently and waiting for instructions. The waterproof, heavily padded bag had protected its contents well.

As if responding to his internal pleading for more light, dawn cracked over the horizon. The thick canopy had canceled the gradual shift, making the change all the more startling, leaving him concerned by how much time had passed. Mina gasped, a shocked little sound that surprised everyone. Basheba raised an eyebrow.

"Sorry," Mina said sheepishly. "I just didn't know you had that much scar tissue."

Basheba gave the girl a thumbs up and forced out, "Brilliant bedside manner."

"I'm going to be a surgeon. My patients will be unconscious."

The soft chuckle brought a sharp spasm of pain. Cadwyn took the opportunity to sink the needle into her skin, knowing the painkillers would take effect soon enough. Of course, Basheba was impatient, and insisted he start stitching her up straight away. As hard as she tried, she couldn't keep in her first gasp of pain. It took Basheba, Mina, and Ozzie working in unison to keep Buck from taking his head off.

"Did I drown?" Basheba asked.

Cadwyn forced himself to hold her gaze. "No, just hit your head."

The lie hovered between them, known by both sides and welcomed far more than the truth.

"Thank you," Basheba whispered.

She didn't say another word while he stitched up her wounds and wrapped her in long lengths of gauze, hoping to give her bruised ribs some support. All the while, she patted Buck, soothing the dog as much as herself, and watched the sun rise. Cadwyn didn't buy it for a second. Knowing how much pain she was in, when the time came, he refused to put up with any argument.

"Piggyback or bridal carry?"

Basheba's brows furrowed. "Say what now?"

"If we're going to keep going—"

"Why wouldn't we?" Basheba cut in.

He ignored the distraction and continued. "You're going to need to rest. I'll carry you until we get there."

She arched one eyebrow. "Are you in any condition to do that? Your leg."

His own chuckle surprised him. "A Chihuahua would weigh more than you. So pick a style, Bell, and let's get a move on."

The following moment of contemplation had way too much mischief in her eyes for his liking.

"Piggyback. That way I can still shoot arrows. You did save my bow, right?"

Seeing how happy she was to be reunited with it, he decided to add, "But you lost your bag."

It hit her like a lightning strike. She started patting her pockets, drawing out each ring to hurriedly count and recount them.

"Twenty-six," she breathed. "Oh, thank God."

Cautiously, he ventured to ask if she was okay, knowing how limited her possessions were. *She doesn't keep a thing she isn't attached to.*

"I have Buck, I have my parent's car, I have the rings," Basheba said. "Nothing else matters. Although, it's going to be a bitch to get a new driver's license."

"We have our crosses to bear," he smiled.

Getting her onto his back was easier than he had anticipated. She scrambled up and wrapped her limbs around him as if she wasn't injured at all. Still, he was careful with her, trying to keep her from being jostled too badly.

"You better not drop me," Basheba said.

"I won't."

"Because I can die from falling from this height," she quipped. "I might need an oxygen tank. You're tall, is what I'm saying."

"Duly noted." He smiled, happy that, despite the pain and fatigue, she was at least in good humor. "Now, which way do we go?"

They followed Basheba's orders for the next few hours, each one of them keeping a careful eye for the snakes. At times, Basheba would wilt, slumping against him with her head propped up on his shoulder, hovering on the edge of sleep. Wanting to give her as much time to rest as they could, they started asking for landmarks rather than having her keep constant vigil. She knew the route like a well-worn trail.

Ozzie had been the one to put their dread into words. "She must have come this way a lot."

Cadwyn turned his head, checking that Basheba was asleep even though he could tell by her steady breathing.

"We can talk about that later," Mina said, adding a reassuring smile when the teen cringed. "Let's just focus on this first."

Their trudge was far longer than Basheba had indicated. Or they were just moving at a far slower pace now. Sunlight filtered through the leaves, turning the air green while still allowing the flowers to almost glow with their vibrance. Cadwyn caught himself stunned by the beauty of it all. Mina proved to have a talent for spotting the landmarks Basheba anticipated. *There's no way on earth that tree looked like an elephant.* When they reached the last marker, Basheba had begun to snore. Even so, she instinctively clutched her bow, her fingers clenching when Ozzie stirred her.

"Is that the cat eye stone?" Mina asked in a whisper.

"Where?" Cadwyn asked.

Mina pointed to a tangle of tree limbs that formed a vaguely oblong shape.

"Yeah, that's it," Basheba mumbled.

Cadwyn blinked. "That's not even a stone. How...?"

"Put me down," Basheba replied, tapping his shoulder in impatience. "It's just over that ridge."

A silent conversation passed between Mina and Ozzie in a single glance. Eventually, the teen ventured.

"Do we have to go through the orchard?"

Basheba stared at him. "How lost are you? No, we're coming around the back. The orchard will be on the far side of the house."

Cadwyn couldn't fathom how they had managed to pull off such a maneuver while moving in relatively straight lines, but he didn't comment on it. The Witch Woods weren't beholden to the same rules as the rest of the world. *Maybe that's why Basheba's so good here,* he thought. *She can find sanity in madness.*

He crouched low, biting his inner cheeks against the pain rattling through his leg, and let Basheba slip off his back. She stumbled for a bit but soon found her footing. All the while, the bow remained tight in her grip. A low, whooping whistle instantly grabbed Buck's attention.

"Recon," Basheba whispered.

Buck took off up the hill like a shadow, silent and swift. The moment he entered the shrubbery, Cadwyn lost track of him completely.

"What kind of training have you put your dog through?" Mina asked.

"The right kind," Basheba replied.

She hugged her ribs with one hand while she waited for the dog to return.

"How is he supposed to express any relevant information?" Mina pressed.

Heaving a slow breath, Basheba started to dig in the dirt with the tip of her bow. Making three squares, spaced a few inches apart, almost in a triangle configuration. She cut a line between her feet and the squares, and an arch over the top. Cadwyn craned his neck to study it.

"The Bell property?"

She started by her feet and worked her way up. "The ridge. Slave quarters and barn. Ranch home. Orchard."

Buck returned as silently as he left, a small tuft of fur nipped carefully within his jaws. After lavishing him with attention, she got around to taking the fur, holding it up to study the tuft carefully.

"What's that?" Ozzie asked.

"Goat hair," Basheba said.

"That doesn't sound too intimidating," Mina said.

Basheba shrugged one shoulder. "That depends on the size of the goat." Gingerly getting onto her knees, she regained Buck's attention and presented him with the tuft. "Where are they? Hey, gorgeous? Where's the goat?"

Buck grumbled for a moment then snapped his jaws about the fur.

Cadwyn, Mina, and Ozzie all watched in stunned silence as Buck dropped the slobber-soaked tuft onto the ground by the slave quarters.

"Good boy," Basheba praised, vigorously rubbing his neck. "You're the best boy ever."

Out of the corner of his eyes, Cadwyn noticed Mina's mouth drop open, and he quickly grabbed her wrist. There wasn't time for the questions they all had.

Basheba was oblivious to the interaction. "Anything else?"

Buck scraped his paw in the area between the back of the slave quarters and the ridge, gouging deep grooves with his nails.

"What does that mean?" Mina asked.

"Something's there."

"What?" Mina pressed.

Basheba finally looked at her. "How do I know? Come on, we should be able to get a decent peek from the hill."

They all wordlessly followed in her footsteps, careful not to make too much noise, and dropping to the earth when she did. Crawling on their stomachs, they slipped under a shrub and reached the tip of the ridge. Cadwyn froze. The run-down Bell property stood as a dark figure embossed upon a vivid world. The lush orchard framed it, thankfully too far away for him to see the hanging corpses. His eyes didn't linger on it. The herd of goat-men instantly grabbed the full focus of his attention.

They stood seven feet tall, huge, imposing, ungodly creatures. A mixture of goat and man, their ink-black horns rose like twin spikes from their heads. Each trod of their cloven feet created a resounding thud that Cadwyn felt rumble through his stomach. *Devils.* The thought slammed into him, robbing him of his breath and leaving him trembling. They were biblical devils.

"Oh my God," Mina whispered.

It was the first time Cadwyn had ever seen the teenager cross herself and he wondered how deep her religious belief went.

"What are they doing?" Ozzie whispered.

They all watched as the devils lead a snow-white bull into a red patch of earth. Each one took a leg while another gripped the head, and they all pulled. The bovine roared in pain as its flesh severed. Cadwyn twisted, hiding his face in his shoulder, as he covered Mina's and Ozzie's eyes. There was no escaping the pop of joints, the wet tear of skin, and the sudden silence.

"Whitney gave one of Katrina's sacrifices," Basheba whispered. "Who do all these others belong to?"

Gathering his fortitude, Cadwyn turned back in time to see some of the devils dragging the hunks of meat to the barn while another led out a new bull. The process began again.

"We're going to have to get past them to light the house on fire," Basheba said.

She scurried backward, leaving Cadwyn to urge the others out of their shock. Once they were all safely within the trees, Basheba took Cadwyn's med-kit and began to rummage through it.

"They did it with their bare hands," Mina whispered. "How do we fight something that strong?"

"We survived a giant spider," Ozzie offered.

"You two aren't fighting anything," Basheba said absently. Cadwyn inched closer to see what had her attention. "Cad, Buck, and I will handle that. You guys just focus on setting the fire and burning that place to ash."

"How are we supposed to do that?" Ozzie asked. "Even your lighter will be drenched."

"That house is all dry wood. It'll go up easily enough. You just need a spark," Basheba replied.

"I don't have any matches," Ozzie said, turning to Mina. "Do you?"

Basheba passed Cadwyn a couple of small bottles of black powder. "Potassium permanganate. It's a water purifier. What of it?"

"Do you have any sugar?" Basheba asked.

Ozzie sat across from Basheba, his arms wrapped tight around himself and Mina pressed close to his side.

"Why would there be sugar in a first aid kit?" Ozzie whispered.

"If diabetics have a sugar crash," Mina replied, her voice just as soft.

Cadwyn was taken aback when Basheba beamed up at him, displaying a half dozen sugar packets.

"Your kit is awesome."

He preened, glad to have someone appreciate it.

"All right, kiddos, listen up," Basheba said. "The first rule of arson is to have fun and be yourself. The second rule is to know your chemistry. Potassium permanganate and sugar. Mix it together on a solid surface. Rub the hell out of it and you've got yourself a spark."

"What is with you and fire?" Cadwyn mumbled.

Basheba ignored him, passing the sugar packets to Mina.

"Do a few different spots—don't block the door—and run like hell. We'll buy you as much time as we can."

"What's our exit strategy?" Mina asked. "I don't think the devils are going to just let us go."

"We won't give them a choice," Cadwyn said with fake bravado, not because he felt any ounce of confidence, but because he knew the teenager needed him to.

"I've got a few arrows left. Buck's got his fangs. Cadwyn has my knife," Basheba smiled.

Mina wrestled in her still damp jeans pocket to pull out a small Ziplock bag of her salt powder.

Basheba's grin lingered somewhere between bloodlust and excitement. "What more do we need?"

CHAPTER 19

Ozzie swallowed thickly, trying and failing to slow his rampaging heartbeat. Despite Basheba's relaxed dismissal of the situation, she chose a methodical approach in preparing for the encounter. She had watched them for at least an hour, her eyes sharp and her focus unshakeable. He had never seen anyone be so still and utterly silent for so long. More than once, he had snuck a look at her chest to check that she was still breathing.

At last, she had slithered back, and another meeting had taken place. Out of all of them, Mina was both the most surprised and the most grateful for Basheba's care. He found it remarkable how relaxed Mina became when presented with a plan. Even if it wasn't a good one. It was the process that seemed to soothe her. That, and the illusion of control.

Once more using her dirt diagrams, Basheba explained her idea with brisk efficiency and a disturbing lack of sarcasm. While they knew the demons were big and strong, they had no way to account for their speed. Basheba's plan, unsurprisingly, was an ambush filled with chaos.

"I can hit a few with arrows from over here," she said, pointing to the far side of the yard, opposite the barn and the paddock holding the sacrificial bulls. "One or two. Just enough to draw interest to me, giving Cadwyn and Buck time to slip around the back of the barn and into the bull paddock. If they're anything like Whitney's, they'll be hostile enough that Buck can easily get them to stampede. Cad, all you have to do is open the gate and get out of the way."

Cadwyn nodded.

"I mean it. If you get gouged by a bull *again*, I'm going to have to laugh at you. A lot. I will say cruel things that will haunt you until your dying day. I don't want to be that person. Don't make me that person."

"I'm flattered you're so worried about me," Cadwyn said, flicking his gaze up to meet hers.

"Did you listen to what I just said?"

"For you, that's practically fussing." His smile fell a little as he added, "Will Buck follow my command? He doesn't really respond to anyone but you."

Buck sat at Basheba's side. He hadn't left more than an inch between them since they had dragged her from the river. Warmth radiated from Basheba's eyes as she looked down to find the dog still watching her. She spared him a pat.

"Just tell him to come to me. It doesn't matter if the bulls flee from him or chase him, it'll work the same. They'll come out and cut across the yard, right through the goat-men. In the chaos, Mina and Ozzie can get to the house."

"How can you be so sure that's the path the bulls will take?" Mina asked.

Ozzie glanced at her, not sure if she was serious. "The way it's all set up, the buildings will act as a funnel."

"But once they're past them?" Mina said.

"That spot is the flattest bit of earth. Cows don't stampede up hills if they don't have to."

Tapping the ends of her hair against her mouth, Mina studied the dirt diagram again. "How can you be sure? I know you're from Texas, but you're old money."

"And a lot of that money is from cattle." He was almost offended by the way the others stared at him. "Granddad still has a ranch. Several, in fact." They still looked unconvinced. "I used to compete at steer wrestling."

Basheba cocked an eyebrow.

"Okay, they were calves, but I was little, too." He hunched his shoulders defensively. "I prefer barrel racing. It's closer to polo."

"There's the posh," Basheba chuckled.

Ozzie wasn't able to decide if he was offended or not by the time Basheba moved the conversation along.

"The goal will be to get them into the woods," she said.

"For your booby traps," Mina said. Not a question, but a statement.

The blonde smiled. "*Our* traps. Ya'll gonna learn what your mama should've taught ya."

"We don't have enough knives," Ozzie said.

Ozzie didn't know what to do with the look Basheba threw him. "Aw, aren't you just the runt of the litter, chewing on electrical wires."

"Are," he stammered, his brows knitting, "are you calling me inept, stupid, or cute?"

"Yes," Cadwyn answered for her.

Somehow, the older man had mastered a tone that both placated Basheba and got her back on track. Ozzie added 'the tone' to the list of things he needed to learn.

"The vegetation is thick there. Sturdy enough to ensure their height and strength aren't such a clear advantage anymore. If they get the upper hand, I'll lure them back around toward the river."

Ozzie worriedly caught Mina's gaze, and they both turned to Cadwyn.

"Are you sure you're up for that?" he asked for them.

"Look at the way they're built," Basheba said, studying the crude map. "They're not going to be great swimmers. I can outpace them across the river and let the *Mahaha* deal with them."

Mina's concern faltered under her sudden desire for knowledge. "Are you sure they'll fight?"

"If they don't, they'll die," Basheba smirked. "There's a reason why we didn't hear so much as a bird in its territory."

For a moment, Ozzie tried to remember that bit of the hike, but it was soon cast aside for the issue at hand.

"Aren't you afraid of water?" he blurted out, hurriedly adding, "and your ribs are bruised."

"If I couldn't do it, I wouldn't have suggested it," Basheba said with an inch of ice caking her words.

"We'll hold everything down out here," Cadwyn cut in, his voice a soothing balm to Basheba's. "You two just focus on each other and setting the house on fire."

Basheba hurried on. "Reminder: secure your exit strategy. House fires spread *fast*. A tinderbox like that is going to fill with a lot of smoke. It should give you enough cover to sneak out. By that time, they should be trying to save the barn, and you'll be able to make a beeline to the ridge."

"Out of curiosity—"

"Are you motivated by anything else?" Basheba cut off Mina.

The brunette continued on, "Why do you think they'll go to the barn?"

"Because they need the carcasses," Basheba said, absently patting Buck as he nosed at her shoulder.

Ozzie couldn't stop himself from wondering, *Is he really that big of a dog, or is she just that tiny of a girl?*

"If the ritual was over," Basheba continued, "they wouldn't be storing them. Katrina wants them for something."

"Right," Mina said.

There was little to discuss after that and, soon enough, Basheba was teaching them how to set up the traps. They worked in the deeper parts of the woods and, shielded by the vibrant leaves and wildflowers, Ozzie almost forgot what was to come. Basheba kept the ones closest to the homestead for herself. Once they had returned to the ridge, Basheba had told them to be ready, and had slipped with Buck and Cadwyn into the plant-life.

Mina was close to Ozzie's side, her steady warmth offering some measure of comfort. They had divided the sugar and potassium permanganate between them—a desperate bid to ensure that either one of them could start the fire. Unsurprisingly, Basheba had snatched up the last couple of bottles.

"I didn't mean it to end up like this," Mina whispered. "I'm sorry."

"Don't count us out yet," Ozzie replied.

He reached out and took Mina's hand, giving it a reassuring squeeze. *Whatever comes, we're in it together.* She squeezed his hand back just as the first devil fell. A flaming arrow protruded from its shoulder, the flames quickly spreading across its wiry fur. It released a feral, inhuman cry. The trees shook as it fell to the grass, rolling and thrashing to put out the crackling flames. The other devils turned, snouts rippling in silent fury. The next arrow struck one in the neck. It went up in flames just as fast as the first.

Buck's bark was overshadowed by the infuriated bellow of the bulls. The ground trembled. A stream of pure white bovines exploded from between the houses, following the black blur of Buck's body.

"Go," Mina and Ozzie said at the same time.

Side by side, they burst free of the trees. Everything happened at once. Colors flashed and sound clashed together under the stench of burning flesh. Buck appeared out of nowhere. He cut through the group, the spikes of his armor slicing deep into the goat-like legs of the devils. Inhuman screams rang in Ozzie's ears. The newest bull being lead to their slaughter huffed and bellowed in the chaos before charging blindly, gouging anything and everything within reach.

Blood drenched the grass and flashed across Ozzie's vision. He caught sight of Basheba racing toward them. She seemed intent on one of the burning remains. Buck held the devils off long enough for the small woman to rip one of the horns free of the carcass. The combination of the dangerous spike and her small stature gave her an unpredicted advantage. She could duck under the devils' muscled arms to quickly strike at their fur-covered legs, finding the joints and bringing them down. Buck was on them once they hit the ground. He was just as efficient as his owner as he clamped down on their necks, squeezing until skin and bone gave way.

A bellow made Ozzie snap around. A devil charged toward them, its inhuman mouth curled in fury. Cadwyn charged to meet it. Just before impact, he ducked his shoulder and threw himself into the creature's legs. They both toppled to the ground, grappling with each other, the hunting knife flashing in the noonday light.

"Cadwyn!" Ozzie screamed, trying to get back to him while Mina kept pulling him forward.

Cadwyn curled his body to drive both of his feet into the devil's barrel-like chest. It brought just enough distance that he could swipe the hunting knife across its throat. Blood gushed from the slit. Ozzie began to shake so hard he almost lost his footing. The copper stench burned his nose and made him gag.

"Stay with me," Mina begged.

The white bull charged before them, blocking their path for a moment before a devil caught its attention. Mina's hand tightened on his until the bones felt as if they would break. They barreled through the back door into the Bell family farmhouse. Suddenly immersed in shadows, Ozzie strained to see. The situation got worse when Mina slammed the door shut and threw herself against it. Ozzie ran back, adding his weight to the wood in a desperate attempt to keep the devils out while Mina struggled with the Ziplock bag of salt.

The door turned into splinters under the creatures' hands, as if they couldn't be bothered to push their way inside. Through the gaps, Ozzie saw how much the fire had spread. It was getting dangerously close to the barn. Basheba and Cadwyn had fallen back to the forest. At least, he hoped they had.

Mina slashed the bag down like a sword, spreading the salt and sealing the doorway. The devils seemed to vanish. The resulting silence had them staggering back.

"Did it work?" Ozzie whispered. "Or are they messing with us?"

Mina blindly groped for his arm as her gaze darted around the room, trying to catch sight of where the devils had gone. "Start the fire."

The unholy creatures' first strike burst a hole through the wall. Blood gushed through the gap, splattering across the room, the brilliant red consuming Ozzie's vision. A copper stench flooded his lungs and made him gag. It left him sick and dizzy and choking on his screams. The devils began to rip the walls apart, tearing into the wood like it was soft flesh.

"Ozzie!"

The desperate cry snapped him out of his fear. Mina was next to what had once been the kitchen table, hurriedly working with her powders. He rushed to the nearest corner, fumbling with the items Basheba had given to him. It took a moment to find a broken stick to mix the substances together. He rubbed hard. Nothing happened. Horns crushed through the wall. Smoke poured inside, blacking the air until his eyes stung. Each new assault brought more blood and smoke. He couldn't breathe.

Come on, come on, come on, he chanted endlessly. Stirring and rubbing. The trembling of his hands almost made him drop the stick.

"Come on," he begged. *Basheba got this to work with an arrowhead and a rag. You can do it!* "Please."

A soft gasp and a small plume of smoke puffed out of the mixture. He leaned closer, trying to see if he had finally succeeded. The sudden flash of fire singed his face. He reeled back, staring in shock. His scream of victory caught him off guard.

"Ozzie!" Mina snapped.

"Right."

Riding the high of his success, he picked another spot. It was easier to get the second one going. Then the third. The walls trembled around him, creaking and groaning as the house began to breathe. Warm air rushed down the chimney, bringing with it a cloud of ancient ash. The air caught the fire, feeding the flames. It barely took a second for the walls to ignite. Red-hot flames raced across the walls, growling like a living beast, building to a blinding light.

The shadows pulled back to reveal the house in its entirety—the remains of a brutal history, a singular moment in time preserved within the decrepit walls. Everything was there—a table set for dinner, toys still spread out before the fireplace, a book open and waiting for its owner to return. Nothing had been packed. Nothing had been taken. *Everyone fled for their lives.* Another roar and the room became an inferno. Ozzie staggered back, his arms lifting reflexively.

"Front door!" Ozzie called to Mina.

She nodded her agreement but waited until he was halfway there before darting forward. Finally, the devils broke through the back door, charging in to hunt them down. Ozzie ripped open the front door to come face to face with another of the creatures. He screamed and fell back a pace. Mina skidded to a stop, her eyes wide, a devil looming behind her. Ozzie tackled her to the floor, crushing the air from her lungs as the devils collided into each other above them. Blood and fire filled the house, both increasing as the building itself continued to breathe.

The house is trying to kill us!

Mina crawled out from under him and latched onto his arm, pulling hurriedly until Ozzie broke into movement. Roof beams crashed down around them, gouging holes in the walls, and bringing the ceiling down in flaming clumps. There was too much smoke to see, too much heat to breathe without scorching their lungs. But Mina's grip was sure and her stride purposeful.

Fresh air struck him like a physical blow. Greedily, he gasped, only for his lungs to protest and throw him into a coughing fit. Blinking away the tears that welled in his eyes, he looked back to see the Bell ancestral home completely engulfed in flames. He staggered along behind Mina, mystified by the sight.

Cadwyn was the first to find them. Battered, cut, and huffing, he ushered them back up the ridge. Basheba stood at the peak, Buck curled around her legs. She only had a few arrows left. By the time they joined her, Ozzie couldn't walk another step. He dropped onto his knees, panting hard, head low. The screams of the beasts had faded away to be replaced by the crackling of the homestead.

"They're gone," Cadwyn said. More of a question than an observation, as if tempting anyone to correct him.

"Is that it?" Mina asked, far more excited. "Did it work? Is it over?"

"We won't know until the next Harvest," Basheba replied breathlessly.

Ozzie slumped to the side and glanced back. His stomach dropped. "Um, guys? Should the fire be spreading that quickly?"

The flames had reached the orchard, spewing a tunnel of smoke into the air that could rival a volcanic eruption.

"That's gonna draw attention," Basheba said. A smile stretched her face. "Upside, the cult's going to be way too busy to be watching my car. Easy getaway."

The wind shifted and the fire spread out like a swelling pool, steadily sweeping out to the horizon.

"Are we trapped?" Cadwyn asked.

"We're going to have to run," Basheba said. "No, not that way. We're heading to the cliff edge. The one that overlooks the river behind the Witch's Brew."

Cadwyn frowned. "Isaac's café?"

Basheba all but danced with excitement, walking backward and giggling. "Yeah. Some airborne embers are going to find their way over there. And, if there's time, it might make it over to Whitney's bed and breakfast, too. What a series of strange events."

Mina and Ozzie shared a glance, neither one knowing what to say, both just desperate to run.

Cadwyn, however, looked rather amused. He shook his head indulgently as they set off as fast as they could go, propelled by adrenaline and the need to stay ahead of the growing inferno.

"What is it with you and fire?"

* * *

If you enjoyed the book, please leave a review. Your reviews inspire us to continue writing about the world of spooky and untold horrors!

Check out these best-selling books from our talented authors

Ron Ripley (Ghost Stories)
- Berkley Street Series Books 1 – 9
  www.scarestreet.com/berkleyfullseries
- Moving in Series Box Set Books 1 – 6
  www.scarestreet.com/movinginboxfull

A. I. Nasser (Supernatural Suspense)
- Slaughter Series Books 1 – 3 Bonus Edition
  www.scarestreet.com/slaughterseries

David Longhorn (Sci-Fi Horror)
- Nightmare Series: Books 1 – 3
  www.scarestreet.com/nightmarebox
- Nightmare Series: Books 4 – 6
  www.scarestreet.com/nightmare4-6

Sara Clancy (Supernatural Suspense)
- Banshee Series Books 1 – 6
  www.scarestreet.com/banshee1-6

For a complete list of our new releases and best-selling horror books, visit www.scarestreet.com/books

See you in the shadows,
Team Scare Street